By the same author –

Snake

To every thing there is a season

The Release

The Deserter

A Flat Country, with Hills

Visit www.edwardarrunsmulhorn.com to find details of other publications, or contact eam@edwardarrunsmulhorn.com

We go blindly
into the darkness

COLLECTED STORIES

Edward Arruns Mulhorn

Paperback ISBN 978-0-9956341-6-9

ebook ISBN 978-0-9956341-7-6

Available in paperback and ebook format

www.edwardarrunsmulhorn.com

If thought is life
And strength & breath;
And the want
Of thought is death;

Then am I
A happy fly,
If I live,
Or if I die.

The Fly, William Blake

Table of Contents

The Bomb Target

We sat on the dunes at the end of the path, pulling off our socks and our shoes, hiding them in the grass. The beach was almost deserted; a few long bodies of adults lay guard over camps in the firm, dry sand, while children squatted in the furrowed shoreline – in the channels, the rock pools – with buckets and spades. Behind them, the receded sea lay bare vast sand-flats, sliding to a broad horizon, naked, changeless, shimmering. Silver-flecked with shallow pools. Home to occasional blurred black dots: the pencil-marks of human shape, in search of stones and shells. There, too, in the muddled middle-distance, a skeleton of other years, proud yet bleeding in the sand, with barnacles to brace its legs, with rust to clothe its ribs.

There were six of us. We started slowly, tracing the haphazard path of a Frisbee, steering an inevitable course towards the bomb target. The sand was slime; it sucked the toes luxuriously with every step. Shells lay open, like hands to heaven, and sand eels ducked beneath our feet, as we laughed and lost our way towards the broken carcass, which stood alone with its scratched thumbs skywards.

Billy gave me a piggy-back across a waist-deep stream because I wasn't wearing shorts. By the time we were clear on the other side, he and I and Isabella were torn from the other three. I walked between them, while Izzy told us about how to catch flounders with your feet. You wade out into an estuary, then you walk around in aimless circles till you feel one move beneath your toes.

You dig down fast and catch its corners, or plunge a trident through the skin of the squirming beast and the sand above it. Then you throw the fish in a frying pan. It seemed absurd, and so easy – starting upon a hapless beast that wriggled beneath you, stranded in shallows, trapped by the force of your weight.

I looked up. Away to the left Lot's Wife stood, dejected: a tower of rock by the side of the cliff. That poor lonely woman, unknown and unnamed, turned to a pillar of salt.

Then Billy told us the tale of how, a few years before, when they were all ten, he had gone for a walk with a group of friends, somewhere out by that point. They were messing around, with no thought or direction, when they chanced on a patch of sinking sand. It was small and unmarked; it lay wanting and waiting. So they searched around them for seaweed and stones, for drift and objects to feed its hunger – watching detritus gorged by its throat, melting into the curious embrace of the close, consuming sands.

There was a girl who was with them – he had forgotten her name – who stood by the side without joining in. She just stood there beside it, transfixed. Watching it, watching it from the edge; staring into its heart. Then, as Billy turned to hurl a boulder into its barren gut, he saw the girl was standing in it – she was in it up to her knees.

There was panic then, and nobody knew what to do. Someone ran off to get help from the shore, while others reached out for her hands. She didn't sink quickly, but she had boots on her feet that wouldn't come off, and her legs just wouldn't come out. She was standing listless as they yanked at her arms, seemingly sapped of her

10

strength. She didn't speak, she didn't struggle, but there were tears in her eyes. Then, when she was swallowed up to her waist, the coastguard appeared with a couple of men and they dragged her clear with a rope.

We were close to the bomb target now. It was made of ten great hunks of timber, crossed with a rusting iron ribcage. It rose as forlorn as a copse in the winter, blind to its long-forgotten splendor. Dissolving through the course of time as the sea's motion bore it down.

Someone threw the Frisbee at me. I didn't see it until too late, and it sailed right over my head. It glided into a shadowy pool beneath the exhausted frame.

I turned and ran – over the sand, over a few green slimy stones at the foot of the nearest post – into the cold, salty pool.

It was dark inside. I stood for a moment in sightlessness. The wind had all dissolved. The target lay in a screed of water; it was cast proud and huge, it loomed large above the distant sky reflected beyond. I feared I would scrape my feet on its bones.

Outside they were calling to me; they were pointing through the sun to the Frisbee, the wind doing battle with their hair. I waded over and stretched through the shadow. As I did so I saw the face of a child – a young child, white, with tears in her eyes, with slow tears spoiling her featureless face. Her lips were moving, I could hear her speaking – ever so softly saying, repeating, 'don't leave me here, on my own'.

The Trophy

Bill and Edie hung the antlers in the hall beside the kitchen door.

The head gave their house a Highland feel – a sense of wildness and adventure – which was just what it had lacked. The current fixtures on the wall – Edie's plates and Bill's old maps – felt dry, suburban, ordinary; so out of place in Sutherland where they had come to make their home. The antlers would astonish friends who came to visit from the South, and maybe – Edie felt – stoke envy. Bill meantime thought fit to hang his flat cap from the lowest point; he told his wife they should rename their home, and have it called 'the lodge'.

Not that either liked to hunt. They were not even keen on sport. Besides infrequent games of tennis when they were young and newly-wed, their sole pursuit was rambling. Walking they loved with unvoiced passion. Being within, and at one with nature. Feeling its power, its majesty, laid out in proud magnificence before their willing eyes. And they its vassals, bent in homage, basking in its glorious rays. Even as they watched. That was why, on Bill's retirement, they had left the South and moved – to somewhere wild and far removed, where nothing would intrude on them but the sun and the wind and the rain. They came in search of that, not sport. Bill had never fired a gun – not even in his army years – at any living thing.

And antlers weren't a living thing. They may have been so once. Now, though, they had been transformed, transmuted to a sterile state of after-life. Not unlike a bandaged corpse, a dried wild flower, they took a new identity – they were not part of what they were – an object that had once had breath. Bill felt his argument was sound. He would not shoot a deer himself; he would not buy a set of antlers if he saw them in a shop. But, if someone offered them to him, if they were being thrown away, then well, why not, thought Bill.

He and Edic had climbed the hill which sloped up high behind their house, up through the tree-line and beyond. They had scarcely been in Scotland a month, and were still exploring the paths and trails which cut through the bracken and startled the gorse. There, on the border of the estate, they had seen a building standing alone which they mistook for a crofter's hut. A man was sitting by the door, fastidiously sharpening his knife. When they waved to him he beckoned them over, and before too long they were deep in talk – in the history and the mystery of the moor.

The man gave his name as Thom – employed to stalk and mind the deer by those who owned the estate. He had followed his father and uncle before him in tracking deer on this land. Thom knew the hill as if by feel. He could trace on his palm every undulation of every valley which stretched from his bothy, here near the coast, to ten miles west. He knew each tree and burn and rock that lay concealed beneath the tread. He knew each bog, each eagle's nest. He knew each print pressed in the peat; which plants grew where and when they flowered; the name of every fern.

And he knew deer. He knew them well. He knew them individually. He watched them cross the boundary which lay invisibly between the bordering estate and his. He watched them roam across the years; he knew their habits and their age. Unseen, he saw the males mature from bold young stags in bachelor groups to imperial beasts which lorded over a whole harem of hind.

And he shot them. Culled them, was the term he used, as if to smooth the deed. He weeded out the weak and injured; the old, and those long past their prime. Most of the time he was merely a guide, escorting rich patrons up the hill to do the culling on his behalf. They paid him several hundred pounds for the kick of firing a gun. They came from the South, they came from abroad, fired by the thrill of the kill. Whenever Thom steered them towards a deer, whenever they pulled the trigger for him, a bounty was pinned to their bill. Then the corpse was dragged down the hill, and the meat sold off to enrich the fare of fancy restaurants and smart hotels. That was the irony of the stalk: the person who stalked got nothing at all. Just swollen ankles and a cartridge shell. They even had to pay ten quid if they wanted to keep the head.

Ten quid!

There, leaning up against the wall, Thom pointed out a pair. Ten quid someone paid him to chisel those off. And the bastard hadn't even come to claim them. Too stinking rich to care. The shame was that they were very fine antlers. They had twelve points, well-proportioned and clean, from a beast which weighed over fifteen stone. Thom remembered it well.

Bill and Edie were invited to look. The antlers had been removed from the head, and were joined by no more than a piece of skull. A bone that was white and polished,

14

like stone. Neatly extracted and clinically clean. So far removed from the living thing that it didn't seem to be wrong.

So what was Thom to do with them? Thom grunted his dismay. He supposed they would stay there and rot down to nothing. Unless they fancied the antlers themselves? Would Bill and Edie like them?

A short while later the couple departed, clutching their unexpected prize.

~

Two natural holes were sunk in the bone. All it took was a couple of nails, and there was their trophy, standing proud, firmly fixed to the wall. Bill and Edie were both quite pleased. Both were secretly overjoyed, though they couldn't articulate why.

That night, after Edie retired to bed, Bill stood in the hall and pondered over what he should put on the points. He had hung his flat cap and a long woollen scarf. But perhaps he should drape his coat. Or maybe just leave the antlers bare. Giddy with new-found interest, Bill's mind raced with idle fancy. His breathing slight, his heart rate fast – the blood pulsed through his arteries. He checked his feelings purposely; he forced his eyes and his thoughts away. Tomorrow he would experiment. He would tease this pleasure out.

Turning off the lights downstairs, Bill glanced back at the patchy darkness, seeing the sharp, misshapen object growing at angles out of the wall – awkward and skeletal – caught in the wash of a spectral moon.

~

Shortly before the creep of dawn, Edie and Bill were stirred awake by a curious low, round, hollow moan. More melancholy than Highland cattle. A sound that was rich and bass and dense. Piercing the walls of their sleeping fortress, vibrating around their barren room.

Again, and yet again. The sound.

Protected by the grey of night from the fear of each other's uncertainty, they lay in bed and did not move. They did not think to speak. They lay in the dark, with their blind backs facing into the other, as if desiring to seem asleep.

~

The next day they spent alone, hugging their silence like secrets, close. By nightfall their solitude stood in between them – it had grown to a cold and piercing pain which sliced straight through their fragile bodies, stripping raw the skin. In an effort to heal the unmentionable wound, they decided to treat themselves to a meal. They drove into town, parked their car in the street, and were crossing the road towards a restaurant when the stalker spotted the pair.

Thom, fired by several drams of Scotch, intercepted them before they could retreat. He snatched at their arms and pulled them towards him, as if keeping his confidence close. Had they heard it last night, that solitary beast, wandering down through the trees? What a fuss it was making – coming so low to bellow despair, depriving the village of sleep. Thom laughed. He thought it might have been their own stag, that had found a way to escape; that had found the means to unhinge itself from their wall and bolt away in the night – wandering wild on the bleak hillside in the early hours before dawn.

As swiftly as they deemed polite, Bill and Edie bade farewell on the pretext of needing to eat. The night reared up before them, hard and black. The sky hung close – timeless and endless – sucking life from the lights of the town, splaying webbed fingers over Thom's moor with the certainty of a shroud. The moon and a few transparent stars stood frosted in the void.

Through the doors of the restaurant a welcome stream of heat and light bade them enter. The two sat in silence; they were happy to cradle their loneliness in the easy banter of the busy tables bustling with noise to their sides. Neither Bill nor Edie were superstitious, yet both were caught by a curious thought – a thought which rose from the pits of their stomachs, coaxed by the chatter and the warmth and the light, till the thinking of it became a reprieve – an admission that both felt thankful to make. The stark and distressing revelation that the wretched stag had come down from the hill in search of the antlers torn from its skull.

Neither husband nor wife shared this vivid image, nor mentioned it to themselves. They persuaded each other in their own minds that the beast which once had possessed the antlers was being served as a stranger's meal. No, their logic was more remote; it was still more dispersed from their guilt. The antlers were detached from the beast; they were wholly removed from the stag.

The antlers were no more than a symbol; a remembrance of stag, a tribute to deer. They weren't a part of life or death; they weren't a part of deer at all. In the close confines of the peopled restaurant, surrounded by a confusion of voices, a distortion of truth interwoven with lies, Bill and Edie suppressed the whisper that fingered into their souls.

By the end of the meal their bellies were full; their conversation revived. Thom was forgotten, as was the sound that was spread with the dawn, that punctured their home and carved into their brains as they slept. And the antlers, too, were a part of that dream.

Flushed and glowing with warmth and wine, Bill and Edie fell back on the night, threading their way through the pools of light which spun from the windows of shops nearby. The street was home to familiar objects: post boxes, litterbins, street lamps. For the first time since they had moved to Scotland these mundane idols of their past were a comfort to shield themselves from the night.

Bill started the car. He drove down the silent road till they slipped into the sheath of murmuring blackness, and began to weave a path through the trees. The beam of their lights threw up before them the regular pattern of urgent white lines, marked down the spine of the road. To their sides, in the sudden fringe of that light, the giddy spectre of endless trees dashed back into eternal shade. The night, impenetrable and immense, leant its weight against the skin of their shallow, half-lit world. Closer, yet closer, the dark bore upon them, stealing around the sides of their car, stifling the stale air within.

Bill hit the brakes suddenly, violently, pulling the car to a halt.

Thirty feet in front of them, facing them and blocking their way, stood a stag. Caught in the curtain of piercing headlight, its body shone an amber-red, and deep, blood-red were its eyes. It stood quite motionless, staring towards them. Not transfixed like a terrified hare, but pensive, unperturbed, and proud. It raised its head an infinite fraction, as if it was wondering where they had come from, and what such bringers of light might be. Then, with deliberate, delicate steps it walked into the invisible trees, and was consumed by the night.

In its place, the empty road, washed by the artificial light, seemed drained and bereft of life. Devoid of any purpose. The engine had stalled. Only the tick of the dashboard clock broke the silence that filled the car, and split the stagnation beyond.

The night as if holding its breath.

Edie and Bill got out of the car. They stood in the space where the deer had been. They squinted in the glare of the beam. Stunned by the brightness they peered up the road. Had it really been a deer they had seen? Was that the creature they saw? Why was it standing in the road, and why did the beast not move? Separately, both were stirred by a similar thought – laden with cautious exultation, with the fierce desire for exoneration. The beast they had seen had antlers.

As their eyes grew accustomed to the pitch, they scoured the trees, expectant, eager. Fearful of catching sight of the stag, there in the deadlight, watching them. Their ears were keen to the depth of silence, wanting and anxious to hear a moan come barking up through the woods.

~

But they did not hear the stag again. Not then, nor in the days that followed. As if stung by a swelling sense of guilt, Bill and Edie found themselves pursuing their walks with greater haste; staying out longer, traveling further; watching, listening, intent. If they were in search of some sign of the stag then they were thwarted in that quest. The moors opened up a treasure of colour which bled with unimaginable beauty for the city-folk who had never seen, nor thought they would see, such gems. Yet deer were not a part of that wealth. Even Thom the stalker was hidden. Had they transgressed some natural code, some law, some elemental custom, they could not have been punished more. All trace of the beast had gone. All save the antlers screwed to their wall, perpetually fixed in their minds. Endearing, but also appalling.

~

Summer had come, and with it the hunting season commenced. Bill and Edie were forced to restrict the scope of their walks now the stalkers were up on the hill. To substitute for the lack of stag, Bill turned to the antlers instead. A fascination was fired within him, like one who arrives at an accident, who is intrigued by another's pain. Now he researched the fate of the stag; he traced the antlers' final journey – sawn and boiled and scraped and plucked from the skull of a living thing. The more Bill learnt, the more he hid his new-found learning from his wife. Edie, he felt, would not want the antlers if she knew what they really were.

But then, he wondered, why did he keep them? What sort of trophy were they?

~

Some while after, wrapped in their wool and waterproofs, prepared to depart on their daily walk, Edie spotted a fleck of fluff caught on the crown of Bill's cap. She stood on the lowest step of the stairs to pluck the speckle away. Closer her fingers came to his cap; closer her eyes to his head.

Then she screamed.

Impulsively, she tore off his cap and scrabbled around in his hair. Bill twisted away, angry, confused. He stooped to retrieve his cap. Then he, too, saw it. There, on the fringe, was a black-eyed maggot, arching its white and puffy body as it wallowed luxuriously in the tweed.

Bill went to the bathroom and washed his hair. He scrubbed his face repeatedly, like a man possessed, unheedful of pain. He felt sick, physically sick in his stomach. He wanted to break from this rancid skin, from this corrupt and decaying corporeal frame. He felt his flesh like a slab of meat stood in the sun to putrefy. He shuddered to think this body was his.

When he came downstairs, Edie was hunched in herself on the step, her figure wrapped closed in a misshapen ball, unwilling, unable to move. Averting her eyes, she pointed towards the antlers fixed on the wall.

Bill followed her hand to inspect the head. The fine twelve points were like delicate fingers, curled to the ceiling, scratching the sky, sprung from the base of the neat white skull. All clinically clean and polished like stone. All, except for the joint on the left, where the antler's root emerged from the bone. There, where the hide must once have been, Bill could discern a clutch of hair. A minuscule, fractional clasp of skin. And clung to the decomposing clod was a moving sea of ecstatic white: a fierce writhing clump of maggots.

~

The strangest thing of all for Bill – after the shock and the nausea, after disgust and the shame – was to realise how alive the antlers must once have been. Of how alive they still were. There was no disguising where they had come from; there was no concealing what had been done. Edie and Bill had nailed to their wall a part of a carcass, a cadaver which was mutilated and maimed.

Swathed in plastic and rubber gloves, Bill took the once-live prize from the wall and threw it into a bag. The antlers – the same which they had embraced in their arms, which had hung with such pride in the heart of their house, which Edie had polished with such tender care – were cast away in a tip. One of Edie's plates was placed in their stead; whilst Bill learned to hang his cap and his scarf on a peg on the back of the washroom door.

That was where it ended for them – this brush with the natural world. It was done.

Though it wasn't the antlers that were diseased, Bill reflected after a while. It was the way in which they hadn't been cleaned, and the maggots which feasted on their decay. If there hadn't been any bloated white bodies, the antlers would still be in his house, taking pride of place. And however shaken he was by the thought of that seething mass, that massive shame, Bill couldn't help but own his regret, to concede how much he missed the head. It had been such a feature; it had given such pleasure. It seemed such a waste that it lay in a tip. Now their home was no more than an ordinary house, devoid of the one thing that made it special. It was dry and dull like that house in the suburbs from which they had dreamt of finding escape.

~

Autumn arrived. The shooting season was growing long. Edie and Bill had seen the fishermen casting their flies on the peat-black waters; they had seen the stalkers climbing the hill; they had heard the haphazard barrage of shotguns discharged from around the loch at dusk. The hill was alive with the bringers of death, with the sounds of death, with the smell. It rolled down the valley and into their home, infecting them both with its stain. Yet they knew this death brought life to the village; it was death that sustained the estate. It brought money, brought work, and brought food. It brought as much as it took away. Life and death. Death and life. And that frightening moment of realisation – that curious state where life meets death – where each stares into the other's eyes.

Bill was out on his own on the hill. He was near the fringe of the rigid tree-line, on the lower slopes where they first met Thom. He had come to escape from his sterile home; from its emptiness, its soullessness. In truth, he was missing the head. If he could secure a clean pair of antlers he was confident he could coax his wife to put it back on the wall. Thom was certain to have another. Thom would have boiled it and scraped it clean. Bill would check to make sure.

There was no one at the whitewashed hut. The door was locked, and the shutters closed. Two pairs of antlers stood by the wall; the smell of blood crept from under the door. Bill walked round the sides of the hut; he screwed up his eyes and scoured the hill. Then he turned his steps towards home.

Two hundred yards down the slide of the slope he came across Thom and a guest. They stood in the heart of a shallow burn, their bent backs facing away. With them, there was a stag. Thom was grappling with its antlers, forcing the corpse across the stream. Its stomach had been sliced open and emptied, its intestines ripped from their still-warm cage and discarded on the wiry heather for foragers to feed. Thom was sliding the awkward body across the uneven face of the moor, leaving a trail of blood in its wake, like a grotesque, lopsided snail.

Bill did not want to look at the deer, but he hadn't the strength to avert his gaze. Its eyes were dead, their fire was gone. Its large pink tongue hung stupidly in the half-open hollow of its mouth. Thom was bringing it back to the hut, back to his abattoir. He was wrestling the body across the moor, while the paying guest looked on.

Thom turned round and saw Bill. He dropped the antlers with a curse, stood straight, and smiled at his friend. Then he raised his hand towards his head, rubbing the blood across his face as he wiped the sweat away.

Bill stared at them, embarrassed, ashamed.

He could have gone to view the beast. He could have helped them cross the burn. He could, if Thom was so inclined, have gone back to the hut with them. He could have watched Thom as he worked – sawing the antlers from the skull, cutting the tendons from the legs, hanging the corpse to let it bleed. He could have shared a dram with them. He could have heard the shooter's tale. He could have grasped the shooter's hand, and shaken it to share his praise.

He could have done. But he could not.

Bill waved; he forced a smile at Thom. He tipped his cap. Then he set off, fast, down the hill.

~

Though Bill said nothing to Edie that day, she noticed a difference, a change in him. The daily walks which led their routine, drew closer and closer about their home. They tightened like a noose. Bill found an excuse why they couldn't go far, they couldn't climb up beyond the trees, they couldn't traverse the estate. Instead, they stayed down low. He steered their walks along the coast, close to the village or through the fields, as if they were held on a leash. She didn't ask him why this was; she feared to ask, to know the truth. She gave him space and time to think. She waited, and she watched.

Then, one day, when crossing a field which led into town – on the flat, in the open, in the height of the sun – they chanced upon a stag. It was standing so still they did not see it till less than a hundred yards away. And now they were standing facing it, caught in the lines of the furrowed land where they thought no deer would come.

Bill and Edie stood their ground. Foolish though they felt themselves, they were afraid to scare the stag by any further move. They knew it would have seen them come; they knew it would have smelt them come. It had the time to run away. And yet it chose to stay. Here, far from the moor, in these tame surrounds. As if resigned to stay where it stood, regardless of how close they came.

It was a well-proportioned beast, with a coat the colour of fading embers. Yet it held its muscular head to one side, rocking it to and fro. It seemed to have shed the wildness within it. There was no depth in its eyes, no spring in its limbs. Though, in its poise, its rigid frame, there was dignity, and grace.

Bill took a step towards the stag. He moved instinctively. He didn't want the beast to start, yet he was sure it wouldn't run. Their eyes had met, and still they met. There was recognition in both.

He came to within sixty yards of the stag.

Then fifty. Thirty.

The creature followed Bill with its eyes, unmoving save for the roll of its head, which it rocked from side to side. There was wisdom in those eyes. There was life, and death, and both were blending, coming together as one.

This was no wild beast. Or, if wild it was, then Bill felt the urge to feel as the stag. To know what it was to be wild, to be free. To share in its agony, and its bliss. To share in its life; to share in its death. To share in its being. To know.

Bill had come to within twenty yards. Now it was only ten.

Then Bill caught sight of the hole in its side, a few inches behind its front leg.

The stag had been shot – it was shot in the stomach – and now it was bleeding to death. It had traveled far; it had come all the way from the moor through the trees, until it was here, in this field. Dying and running, it had covered much ground, eluding the final shot that would kill it, though caught in the motions of death. Death crawled over its faultless body. It shuddered its death, it nodded its death. Death sat proud in its dying eyes. It knew it could run no more. It could not move. Its legs were locked like those of a child that knows without knowing how it knows that even the smallest, the most gradual of movements, is likely to make it fall.

Bill was so near he could feel its warmth. He felt that if he could just reach out – if he could make contact with his hand – his being might be transferred to this beast, to this living carcass before him. He felt that in that moment of touch, the clutter around him would fall away – the façade, the intellect, the self – and instead the creature within would arise: noble and rude, untamed and free, born of both life and death.

There were distant shouts from somewhere behind him. The stalkers had closed on their prey.

Bill turned and saw the blur of two men emerging from a blind thatch of trees. Thom was waving his hands in warning, the other was pointing a gun. Now Edie was also waving at him – Edie who stood in a different realm, detached by a lifetime from him.

Bill looked back towards the beast. It was only him – him and this regal creature before him – populating his world. They stood close together watching the hunters; watching this farce borne out before them. So trivial to those who shared in a secret, to those so at peace with themselves. Those who were breathing both life and death. Life and death. Death and life. And now this subliminal state they had entered, where both were fused as a single being, where each stared into the other's eyes.

Then, as the lesser world coughed and was extinguished, Bill bent forward and touched the stag.

Three Fingers

'I tell you I am Buck Mulligan...! Yes, anything at all… And then they'll come round, will they…? Someone will come round, but not you…? No, of course, if you're too afraid to meet an old man face to face, I'll excuse you… And I'll try not to die in the meantime, and not to get killed. That will make you happy, won't it…? Well, goodbye then. This has been an entertaining conversation…'

The line went dead.

Buck Mulligan listened through the silent earpiece for a while longer, then replaced the receiver on its cradle and stood regarding the contraption in bemusement. It was difficult to process the ridiculous. His mind was wandering chaotically, fluctuating between the preposterous reality of the conversation he had just experienced, and the contrived and implausible world of his fiction, wondering which was the more absurd.

Only he could not reconcile his thoughts. He was so assured of the veracity of his fallacious invention, he was so enthralled by the mechanics with which he had projected himself into his literary masterpiece, that this interpolation of spurious reality – telephones, doorbells, car horns, klaxons, kettles and cats – was unfathomable. Mental fatigue and exasperation swamped his brain with an irresistible acknowledgement that however far one dislocates and estranges oneself from temporal ties, this world – this very real world – indefatigably creeps up and confronts one with its banality, even at the very moment of artistic actualisation.

For had it only been five minutes later, he would have opened his arms to the world, and its telephones and its doorbells and its car horns. Five minutes more and he would have leapt into the street buoyed by deserved high-spiritedness; he would have kissed Mrs Dawkins next door, as she stood interminably on her stepladders destroying her hedge; he would have made sense of the insanity propelled down the phone; he could have proclaimed to the world – 'It is done!'

As it was, such prefiguration was presumptuous; his mental exertions must continue still. Though, as Buck transferred his abstracted gaze from his desk to the nearby drinks cabinet, he considered a sample of the latter's contents might be suitable recompense for the persistent procession of perfunctory calamities which seemed to accost him.

The ice embraced a splash of cherished gin and a slice of smiling lemon, ameliorating his woes. Buck Mulligan returned to his writing desk. Yes, five minutes. No more. There cannot have been more than a dozen delightful sentences to compose. A half page of prose that the academic world would clasp eagerly to its bosom for the next half century; a half page that would warrant the tributes so indulgently and liberally bestowed upon it. Now, even now, before the composition had even seen the light of day, Buck Mulligan felt assured.

And now it was done; it was ended. A brief, inexplicable moment of anti-climax followed in the wake of the final, meticulous full stop. Buck stared vacantly at the remaining blank half page, conscious of its mocking condescension, confident that its virginal lines were not to be despoiled. His exquisite combination of symbols had seemingly been exhausted before its spotless brilliance had been corrupted. Buck heeded its taunt. Yes, there was more he could conjure; he could overwhelm its petty defiance. In a hostile hand he wrote boldly – spelling out each letter methodically, and in conscious capitals – THE END.

And it was, almost at that precise second – just as he was writing the very last letter – that he heard the doorbell ring.

Hell! It was beginning already!

He opened the front door. A man was standing on the top step, staring intently at the buzzer as if mesmerized by its power to summon human form.

'O, it's you. Come in. I haven't seen you for ages. How are you doing…? Can I get you a drink? I've got gin, whisky, or something lighter... There, is that about right...? You've come at a perfect time. I've just finished as a matter of fact… Yes, finished finished. The end. Not that my story has an end… Well, it's difficult to explain in simple terms. I guess it's a philosophical conundrum. Putting yourself in a certain place at a certain time, and then living within it, or trying to extricate yourself from it – starting with me, then the man next door, then some complete stranger, and eventually the reader, struggling to contend with a conceptual construct. As with any fiction, it's set in a parallel world, sufficiently complete and recognisable for the reader to engage with, so he can inhabit it and bring his experiences of the real world to bear. But my world is purer because it is whole and complete. There is no time, no progression, no loose ends. Just an infinite cycle of being. All stories are infinite, in that there are a potentially limitless number of people to read what is written, who will all, through their imaginations, partake of the same experience. They will all become each different character, all become the same character – and all become the same character differently – but in the case of my story they will do so continuously, because there is no closure. Let me put it this way, once the reader engages with the story he is ensnared by it, frustrated by the realisation it is inescapable. The reader is likely to dip into the story, progressively enter it, live it, kick back against it, and finally concede it revolves around himself. Much as he may come to depend on it. It is the infinite nature of the story that keeps him alive, and if he were ever to break that cycle then his literary self would die. To escape that destiny, he may read it many times, and on each reading he may view it differently. But there is no likelihood that different perspectives will bring resolution. No, it is like a sore, an insect bite: the more one aggravates it or is conscious of it, correspondingly the larger and more painful it grows. Ultimately, it's an intellectual game; a riddle in thirty pages. But you can become enthralled by it to the point of obsession. Have you ever noticed how everyone talks and acts similarly, but so few people think the same. The world is in the mind, individuality is the mind, and it is potentially more powerful, more dangerous than Genghis Khan. The mind gives us identity, and it is this identity – in this case myself – which I have transposed to paper. Everyone else is different to me, my mind, my perspective. They may engage with the story differently. They may dismiss it without seeking to understand, they may wrestle with it and escape its claws, or they may flounder within it and drown. But to some extent, they will sacrifice control. They will all become me, and take on who I am. But presumably that's not why you're here… No, I haven't seen your cat. Has she been doing it again…? I'm sorry, you mean your wife… Yes, I did see her the other day. She came over for tea… Well, it must have been Thursday, I suppose, if you really want to know… We had tea. That is the general practice on these occasions… She has been here before, yes. A few other times. Sometimes with you… I can't honestly tell you how often she's been here on her own… It's not uncommon to be friends with a next-door neighbour… Look, I assume you talk to your wife, and she tells you what she's been up to. Being a bachelor, I don't know these things, but I presume that's what you do… Yes, I am a writer. I do have some admirers, that's true… They're people who admire my literature, which is very different to what I think you are insinuating… Look, perhaps we should start again; it's been a curious day. I can't say I understand what's going on… Just before you came round, I was rung up by some madman – someone who thinks he's a policeman – who looked at me through the window then ran away. What sort of madness is that? Come to think about it, he was using the phone in your house. He was on the phone, then he came into the street, then he held up three fingers, then he ran away… No, I'm not bloody making it up! I may be a writer, but I couldn't concoct such ridiculous fiction. So first it's him, charging around in the street; and then it's you, pushing your way into my home and accusing me of – what exactly are you accusing me of? What exactly do you want?'

The world is mad, Buck Mulligan thought. At least, everyone who he had come across today seemed to have lost their reason. What a day it had been! Instead of deriving satisfaction from the pleasurable torment of completing his latest work of fiction, he was being bombarded by the trivial. At the very time when his glorious creation was taking its very first breaths, he was being forced to avert his paternal gaze to contend with a delusional cuckold. It couldn't be real!

Yet it was real. Buck looked over to the drinks cabinet and regarded the man. Here was his neighbour, absorbed in his fury, struggling to make sense of nonsensical thought and translate it into comprehensible speech. A repugnant everyman, married to a bored housewife who divided her whimsical attention between two men – the crass and the creative – who from time to time sought refuge from the world of washing cabbages to enter that of fiction.

Those two extremes had collided. Now his neighbour was here, on his own, trembling with impotent anger. Straining to focus on what to do next, seemingly unable to act.

Though he must have come for a specific purpose. He had come, presumably, to insult, to extract a confession which could not be made, to seek retribution of some kind. If that was the intent, it was not the execution. Instead, his neighbour stood red-faced, silent and stupid, uncontrolled passion consuming his mind. A passion like that which prompts an infant to attack its elder with long flailing arms, a passion past tears and conciliatory bonbons, a passion so vital that Buck was intrigued.

Had it been Buck instilled with such passion, he would have channelled it into creative endeavour. He, a free thinker, a nihilist, a genius, would be able to master such untamed emotion and conjure a majesty from it. That was the inherent difference between them – Buck's capabilities were as transcendental as his neighbour's appeared to be base.

How I hate the man, thought Buck with contempt. A mockery of manhood, a shadow of self, debilitated by the strength of his rage. If even half of what he thought were true, he would summon that fervour, he would focus his hate, he would throw himself at me and kill me.

I could kill him! Silly little shit sitting there in his old man's armchair, looking at me like he's judging me, like he's Mother Superior, like he's God. But what are you? Some fucking academic, some crusty scholarly bastard whose books no one reads and no one understands. Someone who may have been well-known once, but who's now become a no one. Someone who is only a name. A name in a wrinkled old man's body. A name that's dying away. Good bloody riddance! But before you completely faded away, you had to find someone to worship you, someone to remind you of what you once were, someone to make you believe in yourself. And of course you had to find my wife! Silly bloody impressionable woman. She recognised your name. From somewhere in the distant past. And she must have thought you're still famous. So, to satisfy her vanity, she decided to get to know you. And you, you miserable turd, just lapped it up. Finding attention again, when the world had forgotten, was irresistible to you. Don't you realise she doesn't understand a fucking word that you write.

She's not interested in your books, she's not interested in you, she's been caught up by an idea. The idea of writing, the idea of fame, the idea of being creative. You must have known that, but you didn't care. You just wanted the attention. The adulation. You just wanted a woman half your age to stare at you with starry eyes and tell you you were Shakespeare. And she did, and you loved it. You loved it so much that you didn't know where to draw the line. You didn't care about her or me. You didn't give a shit. I could wring your neck, you miserable bastard. I could strangle the life out of you!

In the very act of thinking this, the idea of ending the old man's life seemed thoroughly reasonable to Stan. It was not as if, by killing him off, he would in any way be depriving the world. The old fart was all burned out. He'd spent a month squeezing out a thirty-page story, like a constipated cat. It was time to put him out of his misery. Nobody read his books anymore; he had nothing left to give. And without books he was just a sack of skin containing a jumble of pompous words that nobody knew how to spell. Killing Mulligan would be a mercy, clearing the bookshelves of all his crap, and allowing new writers to breathe. More importantly it would stop Stan's wife from fawning and dribbling all over him at the very sound of his name. And that's what really pissed Stan off. When he thought about all the shit he put up with – his wife going missing, his pregnant cat, the open contempt of Mrs Dawkins – everything seemed to stem from Mulligan. He was the cause of it all. An evil emanating from the old man, directed squarely at Stan. Why Mulligan did so, he didn't know. But Stan felt it his duty, as much as his pleasure, to stop him doing more harm.

Yes, he would do it. He would do it right now. And in recognition of that sudden revelation, Stan felt like dancing, like screaming with joy, like striding straight over to Mulligan and punching the shit out of him.

Feeling that urge, Stan checked himself. He mustn't get carried away. He needed to work out how best to do it, how to make it appear. That level of detail was needed first. Then he could proceed to the deed.

Stan looked around the room, singularly focused on every object as a potential killing machine. A pair of scissors lay unsheathed on the desk, only inches from his hand. It was almost as if the old fool had left them there to tempt him. On a pedestal by the side of the desk was a large black Buddha. What a wonderful way to go – crunching it into the old man's skull whilst the serene Buddha continued to gaze into the distance with seeming approval. Surely that must be the way. Yet it was too easy – too quick and too clean. He might kill the bastard in one blow, and somehow it had to be a slow. Slow, and possibly painful too. Stan wanted to hear the old man squeal, to remind him that behind all these books and words the world itself was real. Tangible, ugly, visceral. Stan needed to bring him back to that, almost as a favour to Mulligan, so the twit could acknowledge his actual death was more than words in a book.

There was also a confession to be heard. Maybe a confession. Something Stan was persuaded was true, though maybe nothing at all. For that reason, too, it had to be slow. To give the man a chance; to explain. And since that was so, though the Buddha was tempting, a knife was a better idea.

And there it was. It was on the drinks cabinet, winking at him as the sunlight sliced off its blade. The cutting edge was short – enough to stop the old fool in his tracks, but not enough to kill him. Plunging it into his shoulder or belly should avoid hitting any vital organs, and prevent him bleeding out. Then Mulligan could have his say before the Buddha came down on his head.

'There's something I want to tell you. Well, it's not really something to tell, it's more like something to show. A trick. A surprise. You see, this little knife here is very deceptive. It almost completely fits in my hand. I think you use it for cutting lemons. And I expect it's good for that. Because though it's small it's sharp enough to get through to the flesh. So, while you probably only use it for lemons, you could also use it for doing this...! There now, I bet you never thought of that... What did you say? I can't really hear you... You're still looking a bit too active for me, so if we just... Come on now; lie still... There we go! Now, that's better... So, let's try and have that conversation again. Tell me what I already know. Get on with it, you obstinate old bastard. Tell me in your own words... No? Not even if I persuade you again...? Very well, let me tell you the story myself. I moved here about three years ago with my wife and my black and white cat. We were all very happy back then. A new house, a new job, potential new friends. A whole lifetime to enjoy together. But then you appeared, and fucked it all up. I guess someone told us who you were, and even though that meant nothing to me, my wife had vaguely heard of you. So, she found an excuse to come round. And you liked that because you'd been forgotten; you were a washed-up writer with nothing left in the tank, and were drinking your life away. So, it suited you both to be friends. She could pretend she knew someone famous; you could pretend that person was you. And to begin with it was quite innocent. She would come round from time to time, telling me what you had talked about as if thinking I would care. But after a while, things changed. I think you got ideas. Not ideas about books and clever words, but man-sized ideas about her. And I think you knew enough about her to know how to sell those ideas in. Well...? Nothing...? A bit more persuasion perhaps...? She began to go out more by day. For part of a day; sometimes for the whole day. Though it was hard to tell because I was stuck in an office doing real work in the real world. Often, when I phoned from work, I found that she wasn't in; when I came back home, I found the cat hadn't been fed. She didn't mention that she'd been out; she didn't mention who she'd seen. But there were clues. Two ticket stubs to a book signing. Who else but you would go there? Then that time – if you recall – I phoned you because my cat was on heat, and my own wife answered the phone. Your phone. Can you imagine what that's like? Knowing you were both here, laughing at me, throwing your shit in my face. I don't care that you gave her chocolates on her birthday, or taught her words that she doesn't understand. I'm just pissed off that you're a miserable bastard. I'm just pissed off you exploited my wife. I'm just tired of all this, you old fart. So, get on your knees and confess. Well...? I can give you as much encouragement as you need. I really don't care anymore… For a man who has usually so much to say, why can't you say a word...? Hey there! Focus on me. Focus on my story, not your fucking story. I'm going to burn yours anyway…'

Stan stood up. He stepped carefully over the various obstacles which had somehow come to litter the floor over the last few minutes. It was done. The old bastard didn't do so badly after all, though he was a bit disappointing at the end. In those final moments it just fizzled out. After all, the old fool hadn't admitted to anything, and you would have thought he would do so having nothing to lose, and presumably being in pain. Why hadn't Mulligan told him the truth? Maybe, through silence, he had. Maybe his silence was his way of saying that there was nothing to say. No defence for a sin that wasn't committed.

A curious thought came into Stan's head. Perhaps he was wrong about the whole thing, perhaps it was all in his mind. It was all a mistake, a fabrication. As elaborate a fiction as one of Mulligan's own. A story invented through idle inference to patch over an imperfect world.

The Buddha winked at him. Stan had forgotten about that completely. The knife had proven so effective that he hadn't needed to call on the Buddha to set Mulligan onto a higher path.

Stan sat down by the desk. For some reason, Mulligan's earlier unintelligible rant had lodged itself in his mind. He was listening to it all, not just as a jumble of words once spoken, but as if Mulligan was alive and speaking it still. Speaking it for the first time. And this time around, it seemed to make sense. He could hear that affected, monotonous voice populating the silent present with words that he first had heard in the past, with words that he feared he would hear in the future, as the dead man's reckonings ransacked his brain, tirelessly, unable to end.

Stan picked up the dictionary on the desk. He flicked over the pages till he came to the word 'nihilist', for such had Mulligan claimed to be. 'Someone who believes that there are no principles or beliefs that have any meaning or can be true'. Then surely it made no difference to him whether he was dead or alive. Surely he would be arguing still whether in fact he was dead. He would still be disputing his current condition, if it were in fact a fact.

Stan prodded the body to make sure. The fact of what was seemed real enough, but maybe not the concept. Mulligan had started writing, Stan seemed to recall, because he desired to live beyond life, to live when other people had died, to project his being into the future, not as a memory but as a person who exists in the present, alive.

Then surely in that he had failed. Stan snatched the written manuscript from the desk, and impulsively threw it into the air, watching the fluttering pieces of paper land on the carpet and dip themselves into pools of clotting blood. He would leave them there, not burn the story, so that at least might live on.

The story would live on, and so would Stan. That was a cause for celebration. He stood to pour himself a drink, reaching for the bottle of gin to top up the glass in his hand. As he poured, he noticed the bottle was shaking, the liquid spilling onto the desk. Only it wasn't the bottle that trembled. It was him, his hand, his whole body shaking. Indeed, the bottle was the only thing that didn't seem to shudder. He put it down forcefully, turning around to confront the room, to see what must be seen.

Yes, it was only him who was trembling; his limbs quivering uncontrolled. Everything else was still. Still and silent. Just as it always had been, just as it had to be. The same as it would have been that morning when the old fool shuffled into the room, when he reached out to turn on the light. The same; surely, as always, the same. This room had outlived its recent owner; this room was still alive. Not actively alive, but with a life which absorbs and consumes the actions of anyone who enters. The lidless eyes of the static Buddha, the waiting typewriter keys. Even that body, with extended arms, as if stretched out in welcome. It had all resumed a sameness again. All placed where it should be, as if it belonged there, set in position with care.

The only alien object was Stan. Of everything that crowded the room, it was he alone that was wrong. Then what was he doing here? Why was he here? He was the only sentient thing in this dust-filled chamber of stunning silence. This breathless sepulchre.

He drained his glass, taking a handkerchief from his pocket and methodically wiping its rim. Then he retraced his steps, wiping everything he had touched, everything which bore his impression, everything but Mulligan's body which lay in the centre of the room.

The pregnant cat was sitting on Mulligan's doorstep. Foolish creature. Didn't it know that it lived next door? Stan picked it up in his arms, looking out across the street to see if someone was watching him. The pavement was bare; there were no cars on the road; the windows around him were blind. He was confident he had not been seen; there was no one to witness him.

He shut the front door and went down the steps. In his mind he counted out the paces between Mulligan's door and his own. He glanced around again. The street was as soundless as Mulligan's house, entirely bereft of life. Not even Mrs Dawkins was there, scowling her knowingness.

He fitted the key in the lock and entered, placing the cat down on the floor, hearing the soft patter of its feet as it ran towards its food. Stan listened out for other sounds, for any sign of life. There was none. He knew himself alone in the house, this house as silent as Mulligan's own, as watchful and patient, as undemanding, waiting for someone to bring it alive.

Again, for a moment, he doubted himself. If his wife wasn't here then where was she, knowing that she wasn't next door. Perhaps her life of unexplained absence, of impatient gestures and lame half-answers, perhaps that life would still go on. Perhaps he had got the wrong man.

Stan stood in the hall absorbing the silence, feeling the stillness wrap round him. He must have thought this next stage through; he must have had a plan. He would have known it would come to this. This moment, when he still had the edge, when he was the only one who knew. They would come to him, naturally, as a neighbour; they would want to interrogate him. They would ask him where he had been, and who he had been with. They would ask him how well he knew the old man next door. They might ask him other stuff too. Stan's trembles had given way to a vagueness. He tried to rehearse his alibi, going over the words in his head. But instead of his voice he could only hear Mulligan, spouting his philosophical crap, drowning out reason with a torrent of sound.

He went to the kitchen and put on the kettle, dropping a teabag into a mug, reaching out for a spoon. Each action conscious, deliberate, as he sought to focus his mind. Kettle. Teabag. Mug. Spoon. So habitual it should have required no thought. Though now it needed such concentration, as he sought to block out the old man's voice as it wove its tendrils into his brain.

Stan fed the cat then went upstairs, the cup of tea in his hand. If he couldn't shake Mulligan when awake, maybe he could lose him in sleep. He got into his pyjamas. He climbed into bed. He closed his eyes; he closed his mind. He lay as still as Mulligan lay – there in the next-door house, on his own – awaiting a similar peace.

Stan woke. At first, he didn't know where he was. This was his room, his bed. He felt it with his hands. His wife was not beside him, and her side of the bed was cold. He listened out for sound through the floors below, but all he could hear through the silent house was the faintest swing of the cat flap. He glanced towards the window. The curtains were still open. Beyond them a bland white sky, the same as when he fell asleep. Seemingly the same. Then he could not have rested long. Though he felt well-rested, still drowsy with sleep, as if he had been asleep for a while. And in that while the old man's voice had faded into a whisper.

A shrill, unwelcome noise cut through the silence. The doorbell. Its insistence suggested an impatient hand. It must have been that that woke him. Stan drew back the duvet and stood up, taking a dressing gown from its hook, and tying it around him as he went down the stairs.

He opened the front door. A man was standing on the top step, staring intently at the buzzer as if mesmerized by its power to summon human form.

'Hello...? Yes, that's right. And who are you...? O. How can I help you? What do you want? I suppose you'd better come in… Yes, I've only just woken up. I've been asleep for ages. I don't know why. I don't usually go to sleep during the day, but I was feeling really tired… Would you like a cup of tea...? Are you sure...? This is the living room. Have a seat… Buck Mulligan? Yes. He lives next door. He's a writer, of fiction I believe. Sorry about the cat. It's pregnant and needy… Well, from time to time. We've had him round for supper once or twice. Poor man lives on his own. And I suppose we've been over there a few times too. You should really speak to my wife. She's out at the moment, but she's the one who knows him. We moved here about three years ago, and since then she's struck up a friendship with him. Nothing dodgy, of course. She's a bit arty, which is probably why they get on, whereas I'm not into books… No, he seems a nice enough guy. But why do you need to know all this? Has he gone and done something bad...? He what?! When, how? That's terrible. Is there anything I can do...? Why would anyone want to kill him? Have you any idea who it was...? Yes, of course, I understand. It's my day off today. I got up, fed the cat, had breakfast with my wife. Then she had to go off somewhere. Said she'd be gone for most of the day. I don't think she told me where. So, I pottered around here a bit on my own. I went into the garden and pulled up some weeds. Then I suddenly felt unusually tired, and since I didn't have anything planned, I just went back to bed. Pretty boring really, and I guess not much of an alibi… I suppose you can check the first part with my wife, but after that no one saw me. In fact, I think it would be much better if you did speak to my wife. She's likely to be more help… You have already? Where is she…? Why's she there? You can't believe she's a suspect. She knew him quite well, as I said, but they got on well. She was kind of devoted to him. An admirer. She must be distraught. When can I see her…? So how long will you keep her there? Is she all right? I think I need that cup of tea after all. You'll join me? I insist…'

Stan stood up and went into the kitchen. It was all so easy, so wonderfully simple. It was all falling neatly into place. Of course, it came as a shock that his wife found the body, but the fact that she did made it perfect. Stan's shock must have shown itself in his face, so he didn't even need to act. And by finding Mulligan she was framing herself, she was raising doubts about why she was there, about how she got in, about the relationship between them.

Based on what Stan was told, his wife arrived just after he left. He only just did it in time. But that didn't matter now because no one had seen him. All that mattered were the facts. She let herself in; she found the body; she screamed and ran out; Mrs Dawkins saw her and phoned the police; they picked her up, and in her condition who knows what she might have confessed. Her fingerprints would be everywhere too. It couldn't have been more perfect. So much so, that despite himself, Stan almost felt sorry for her.

He glanced back into the living room while waiting for the kettle to boil. The inspector was sitting hunched in his armchair, scribbling notes in his pad. There was almost no need to lead him on further; his wife had done all the work. Meanwhile Stan's own alibi was so simple it seemed beyond all suspicion. Now he could simply sit back and relax, watching the farce play out.

Stan returned to the living room, two mugs of tea in his hand. He brought a box of biscuits too, and a couple of slices of cake. He would make this a party, as much as he could, whilst outwardly appearing upset. After all, it couldn't be often that a police inspector was detained by a culprit in his own house, or that a culprit could watch a police inspector implicate his own wife.

The eyes of the uninvited guest suddenly, briefly met with Stan's as he placed the tea on a side tray. His eyes were faintly bloodshot. Over-weary and overworked. The inspector turned back to the jottings in his notebook, scribbling once more in an illegible hand.

Stan observed the man in silence. Analytical, that's what he was. He had all the facts, he had pieced them together. There could only be one conclusion. Mulligan didn't have any friends; he was almost a total recluse. The list of suspects, from the top, must read – Stan's wife, then Stan, then Mrs Dawkins, then, lastly, the cat. There was no one else it could be. And out of all those, only one suspect was real. The one who saw him most frequently; the one who had his key; the one he was probably having an affair with, however improbable that seemed. Maybe that was the fact that perplexed the inspector, as he scribbled notes in his book.

Knowing that he did it, the question is why. What would make him commit such a crime? He's a young man, with his whole life before him. He's got a good job, a loyal wife, a house, a cat, good health. Why jeopardise that? Why throw it away? What madness could have possessed him? It would be different had it been a single blow, such as bludgeoning Mulligan with his own Buddha. That might be put down to rush of blood, for a first offender with no criminal record. Depending on motive, and a lenient judge, it might lead to manslaughter, not murder. But this is in a different league. Twelve stab wounds made to the torso; the laceration of the liver twice; a punctured right lung and broken ribs. This is premeditated, calculated, cruel. And no mitigation of any kind; no record of poor mental health. Just look at him now, sat opposite me, confidently drinking it in. He thinks he's got away with it. He thinks I'm struggling to piece it together. He thinks I think it's his wife. He thinks that by playing the outraged neighbour, I somehow can't see the glint in his eyes that shows how much he is milking this. That is perverse, but it doesn't answer the question as to why he did it. He disliked the old man maybe; they had some kind of dispute; he was envious that Mulligan liked his wife. Perhaps he thought they were having an affair. None of those reasons should lead to murder as heinous and savage as this. But the question of why can wait. The question for now is whether to press him further in the hope that he might confess. That would save time, and upset, and pain. That might cut through his web of lies before they swallow the truth. And in doing so he may tell me the motive without me needing to figure it out.

The inspector looked across at Stan. He was sitting quietly in his chair, a modest, sober, clever young man, so assured and so different from the frenzied killer he had shown himself to be. Were he to confront Stan now, on his own, would the man sat before him remain the same man, or would he revert to the beast?

'I'm sorry to have kept you waiting so long. I have been deliberating, you see. I've been wondering to myself, I've been trying to reason why you killed your neighbour so violently... Yes, I know you did it; there's no use in denying it. I just want to know if you'll give me a statement... No, I wouldn't like more tea. And I'd rather you stayed where you are, in your chair. I'm offering you a chance. I think it advisable that you consider your predicament, that you take up my offer while you can. What you have done you have done, but by cooperating now and in full you may yet avoid the harshest sentence, and put yourself in a better light... Yes, I know you were asleep. When you came to the door, your right cheek bore crease-marks from lying on the pillow, and your arm on the same side was deadened. I don't doubt that you were indeed asleep, but you weren't asleep when Mulligan was killed... I have made you an offer, and I won't repeat it. All I will say, considering you don't know the extent of my knowledge, is that I can tell you quite candidly that I am not only entirely convinced of your guilt, I have definitive proof that you did it. The perfect crime has, in my experience, yet to be committed, and yours – though carried out to your own satisfaction – was decidedly flawed in many respects... Yes, you have said you were asleep, and no, I don't know for precisely how long. But what I do know is that there is a phone by your bed. That phone rang three times today, when you claimed to have been asleep. I'm very surprised it didn't wake you, but the reason it didn't was because you weren't here. You were busy next door at the time. Your wife's car had broken down, you see. So, your wife was phoning to let you know she was taking public transport home. If you check the answering machine behind you, you'll hear her telling you that. I can see the machine is winking at me now, showing the messages are there... Yes, it's possible you are a very deep sleeper, and no one would convict you on that evidence alone. I'm telling you more to set the scene, since you are unwilling to tell me yourself. You wife came home, to this house. She thought she would find you here. She checked the garden; she checked every room; she even wondered if you might be asleep. But you weren't. The house was empty... Yes, I know this is just her word against yours, that she could be trying to implicate you. But allow me to finish, and then decide whether to make a statement or not... Let's feed the cat when we're done... Thank you. So, the next stage requires contextualisation. Your wife and Buck Mulligan are very good friends, they get along very well. That doesn't mean she doesn't love you; that doesn't mean she's having an affair. And that is the saddest part of it all, because I expect you think that she is. No, she visits him to talk books and art. Things that mean little to you or me, but things that are precious to them. And that's no crime. Unbeknown to you, perhaps, she approaches his house through the gap in the hedge which separates your two houses; she enters his kitchen through the patio door which leads to the garden at the rear. That avoids any casual gossip, that avoids the need for a key. So, having found your house was empty, she thought she would go and visit Buck Mulligan, and went round to the back by the hedge. And on this occasion, on looking up, she saw something she hadn't expected to see. She saw you, near the window in his study. The next bit should sound familiar. She saw you sitting at his desk. She saw you reading his dictionary. She saw you with papers in your hand, which you threw up into the air. She saw you pick up a bottle of gin. She saw you wiping various objects before stepping carefully away from the desk and into the depths of the room. Of course, this could still be your word against hers, but forensics are likely to back up her version. As is Mrs Dawkins, who was looking on: who was watching your wife as she watched you. Would you like to make that statement now...? Yes, if you wish to know. Your wife remained in the garden awhile, till she saw you were back and in your own kitchen. You were making a cup of tea. She trusts you, but she was also afraid. So instead of returning home, she crept through the gap in the hedge, then alongside the flowerbed, and let herself in through the patio door. I think you know what she found. She didn't stay long – just long enough to assure herself Buck Mulligan was dead – then she left the house by the front. She knocked on the door of Mrs Dawkins, and from there she phoned the police. We came round, but I expect you didn't hear us, because by then you had fallen asleep – just as you told me – into the deep sleep of exhaustion. And you slept deeply for a long time. Long enough for your wife to give us a statement. Long enough for Mrs Dawkins to give one too. Long enough for my officers to secure the crime scene, to begin a forensic examination. And that is what they are doing right now. And that is why I'm arresting you, for the murder of Buck Mulligan. I would like you to come with me to the station. I would like you to make a statement now. I will call in my officers to escort you. I will close up the house and then come and join you… Yes, if you like, I will feed your cat.'

The inspector stood up. He moved towards the window at the front of the house, and motioned through it, into the street, his eyes still resting on Stan. There was a knock at the front door. The inspector held out his arm, and Stan, unspeaking, followed its arc, being ushered through the door and then down the echoing hall. The inspector reached for the latch. Two uniformed officers flanked the top step. They guided Stan down onto the pavement, and from there to a waiting van. The inspector watched the van drive off, then he closed the door. It was done.

It was done. He leant back against the heavy frame, resting his head against the wood, closing his eyes on the hall. Consciously, he took six long breaths, in through his nostrils, out through his mouth. He was always saddened by solving a murder. There was no satisfaction in finding the culprit; there were no heroics in the arrest. All he could see was what lay in its wake – the lives that were ruined, the scars that were left. The torment, the loneliness, and the tears. It was not just the victim; it was everyone else. It was Stan's wife, Mrs Dawkins, and the people who lived here. All those in the street, who were somehow diminished, somehow deprived of a brighter outcome by seeing done what was done. There is such kindness and greatness and promise in people, yet he only met them when it had gone wrong. When it was too late. When the wrong was done. When hope had already died. Each case he entered, each case he solved, felt like he was being eroded, felt as though a piece of him died. And for what? Such pointlessness to each murder he saw; such pettiness in the deed. Each day, the humanity he encountered displayed its hopelessness and its fear. How hard was it then to harbour hope, to believe that goodness was still alive.

Reluctantly, he opened his eyes. Mental fatigue and resignation swamped his brain in acknowledgement that however much he stayed distanced, detached, the imperfections of this world – this very real world – confronted him on a daily basis, leaving him with their stain and scars, leaving him no time to heal. He felt exhausted. Like he could sleep the same sleep as Stan had slept. One so deep it extinguished dreams. So deep that it snuffed out despair. He wished he could wake up renewed and refreshed, and find it was yesterday.

The cat came up to him, and he picked it up, relieved by the sense he was not alone. There was something else in this room with him, something living alongside him that was unthreatening and mundane.

The cat leapt down from his grasp, purring and padding towards the kitchen. It led the inspector up to its bowl. He could see its biscuits on the counter. He reached over to pick up the bag. As he started pouring the contents out, he noticed that the bag was shaking, the biscuits spilling onto the floor. Only it wasn't the bag that was trembling. It was him, his hand, his whole body shaking. Indeed, the bag was the only thing that didn't seem to move. He put it down with force.

Yes, it was only him who was trembling; his limbs quivering uncontrolled. Everything else was still. Still and silent. Just as he guessed it always had been. Just as it would have been that morning when Stan and his wife came down to breakfast. The same; but now it would not be the same. Stan's wife would return, and the cat would remain, but Stan would no longer be here. And without Stan it was not the same house, it would never return to what it once was. It had lost what it had; it had been defiled. Just as now it was being defiled. For here he was – an outsider, a stranger – stood in their kitchen, feeding their cat, free to do what he pleased. What was he doing here? Why was he here? Standing alone in this silent house, this room as breathless as a tomb, now he had ejected its owner.

He needed to return to the station. There was so much he needed to do. Mechanically, he picked up the cat bowl, washing out the remains of its food. He retraced his steps to the living room, plumping up cushions, straightening chairs, purifying the room. Finally, he picked up his notepad, slipping it into his inside breast pocket alongside a half-dozen pens. Such tiny pages and scribbled words, filled with immeasurable sadness and sin. There was so much hurt within its thin covers. So much hurt so close to his chest. Weighing him, weighting him down.

There was just one more thing he had to do before he left for the station.

He walked to the phone and picked up the receiver. He dialled a number, and heard it ring.

'Hello. Perkins? How are you doing over there? Are the forensics team still with you? Have they removed the body yet...? Mulligan's body. Have the come for it yet...? Perkins? Is that you...? I'm sorry, who am I speaking to? Could you put Graham Perkins on the phone...? He's one of the team I sent over. He should be overseeing the forensics… You can't be there on your own. They can't have finished already… The forensics team… Who is this that I'm talking to...? But you can't be! That's not possible! Stop fooling around. Who is this really...? There's no way on earth you can be Buck Mulligan...! No. Don't hang up. Please. Are you seriously telling me that you name's Buck Mulligan? The writer? Aged 73? Living at 67 Cedar's Drive...? But you can't be. It's simply impossible… Why? Well, because Buck Mulligan's dead.'

'What?! What on earth are you talking about?! I ought to know if I'm dead or alive… Yes, I'm taking this seriously too. Being alive really matters to me. Being dead would matter even more… You've asked me my name, and I've already told you. I'm Buck Mulligan… Yes, there's only one Buck Mulligan a far as I know. It's not exactly John Smith… Yes, I do live at 67 Cedar's Drive, and have lived here for the last twenty years… I'm feeling absolutely fine, thank you very much. How are you doing today...? Of course I can be sarcastic if I want. Now, goodbye… Yes, there is a drinks cabinet beside my desk. There's nothing unusual about that… Yes, there's also a Buddha on a pedestal. Lucky guess… How do you know I've just finished a story?! How can you possibly know that?! No one knows that. I haven't told anyone. No one has even seen it… What do you mean, has it got blood on it? Do you think I've had a nose bleed? Do you think

I go around stabbing myself for inspiration? Are you mad...? Who are you, anyway? You haven't told me your name. Why are you phoning me, and what do you want...? You're telling me you're a policeman? You expect me to believe that...? This isn't Stan, is it? Stan, is that you? Is this your idea of a joke...? You're phoning me from his house?! You're next door...? Then would you mind putting him on to me, so I can have a sensible conversation... You can't. Why not?... He's been arrested?! For what...? For what...?! Now, let's just roll back a bit. I think there's been a misunderstanding, a mix up of some kind. You may be a police inspector for all I know. But tell me this, if I'm dead why am I answering my phone...? Yes, there must be a simple way to resolve it... No, don't come round...! OK, just to the window. Yes... Hold up three fingers? Yes, I'll wait...

'... Hello again... Why were you running away...? Yes, I saw your three fingers. Did you see me...? Good, so you know I'm alive. That's reassuring. Yes, it is me, not someone pretending to look like me... I think we're covering old ground here. I think it's time to hang up... For the last time I tell you I am Buck Mulligan...! Yes, anything at all... And then they'll come round, will they...? Someone will come round, but not you...? No, of course, if you're too afraid to meet an old man face to face, I'll excuse you... And I'll try not to die in the meantime, and not to get killed. That will make you happy, won't it...? Well, goodbye then. This has been an entertaining conversation...'

The line went dead.

I listened through the silent earpiece for a while longer, then replaced the receiver on its cradle and stood regarding the contraption in bemusement. It was difficult to process the ridiculous. My mind was wandering chaotically, fluctuating between the preposterous reality of the conversation I had just experienced, and the contrived and implausible world of my fiction, wondering which was the more absurd.

Only I could not reconcile my thoughts. I was so assured of the veracity of my fallacious invention, I was so enthralled by the mechanics with which I had projected myself into my literary masterpiece, that this interpolation of spurious reality – telephones, doorbells, car horns, klaxons, kettles and cats – was unfathomable. Mental fatigue and exasperation swamped my brain with an irresistible acknowledgement that however far one dislocates and estranges oneself from temporal ties, this world – this very real world – indefatigably creeps up and confronts one with its banality, even at the very moment of artistic actualisation.

For had it only been five minutes later, I would have opened my arms to the world, and its telephones and its doorbells and its car horns. Five minutes more and I would have leapt into the street buoyed by deserved high-spiritedness; I would have kissed Mrs Dawkins next door, as she stood interminably on her stepladders destroying her hedge; I would have made sense of the insanity propelled down the phone; I could have proclaimed to the world – 'It is done!'

As it was, such prefiguration was presumptuous; my mental exertions must continue still. Though, as I transferred my abstracted gaze from my desk to the nearby drinks cabinet, I considered a sample of the latter's contents might be suitable recompense for the persistent procession of perfunctory calamities which seemed to accost me.

The ice embraced a splash of cherished gin and a slice of smiling lemon, ameliorating my woes. I returned to my writing desk. Yes, five minutes. No more. There cannot have been more than a dozen delightful sentences to compose. A half page of prose that the academic world would clasp eagerly to its bosom for the next half century; a half page that would warrant the tributes so indulgently and liberally bestowed upon it. Now, even now, before the composition had even seen the light of day, I felt assured.

And now it was done; it was ended. A brief, inexplicable moment of anti-climax followed in the wake of the final, meticulous full stop. I stared vacantly at the remaining blank half page, conscious of its mocking condescension, confident that its virginal lines were not to be despoiled. My exquisite combination of symbols had seemingly been exhausted before its spotless brilliance had been corrupted. I heeded its taunt. Yes, there was more I could conjure; I could overwhelm its petty defiance. In a hostile hand I wrote boldly – spelling out each letter methodically, and in conscious capitals – THE END.

And it was, almost

The Compleat Angler

Bass. Bass whispers Snead, in the hunched, yellow home-glow of the pub. Bass, he hisses, his breath on Phelps' ear, his words congealed in the close, drugged air. A bass conspiracy.

Yet Phelps is unconvinced. He has only known till now the feel of sea-salt in his face, the throb of the motor, the roll of the boat, the six-hook lines which trawl the coasts for shoals of mackerel. He has only lived till now for cloudy dusk and misty dawn, standing on the silvered bank while casting a continuous fly at salmon which would trek upstream. He has only cared till now to split the surface sheen of lochs with oars to guide a creaking hull to haunts of midnight trout. Phelps has never gone for bass.

Bass, says Snead, caressing the sound, bass is a beast you catch by guile. Bass is the fisherman's dream.

To Phelps the dream seems more a nightmare. Forced to bob in an idle boat in the narrow waters of an estuary – shallow, unblown, unmoving, alone – with nothing to do but watch a line you never trim or reel back in, hoping a fish is foolish enough to take a spontaneous swipe. Where is the skill or adventure in that?

That, says Snead, is precisely it. He bends his body towards the fire, dragging fat fingers through his beard. The single way to catch the beast is to be more boring than the bass.

The following day, with little haste, Phelps ambles down the sea-slick jetty, to take to the estuary in Snead's boat.

The morning sun is bright and sharp; the air is cold, and the water too, as Phelps slips from the lazy mooring, and drifts his boat down the salt-water river, gliding gently from the shore. Phelps takes the oars and makes for the channel, maneuvering round the dormant berths of other craft. The breeze is slight, the shoreline grey; the fields are shadowed in thin mist as he takes the sun upon his back and ventures to the sea.

As he rounds the final curve in the stream the wind picks up; waves crease and thump across the bar, spitting their spume in his hair. Phelps makes for the sheltering cliff which lies on the farther side of the river's mouth, guiding the boat with heavier strokes towards the mottled crags. Here he slackens off the oars, catching sight of the sandy floor and the dancing shadow of his hull, drowned some fifteen feet below, broken by the motion of the sun-smitten sea.

The anchor splits the water. Phelps stows his blades, prepares his line, and points his rod towards the drunken bed which stares back at him buoyantly.

The giddy surface breaks to take his bait. Phelps steadies his weight within the boat, secures the gut and readies the spool, and cranes his neck towards the sea, cautiously searching the liquid world to gauge the depth of his line.

Anchored in the heart of the boat, the boat to the bed, the bait to the brilliant hook, Phelps never moves, he scarcely breathes. Only the regular pound of his heart, the trespass of interest caught in his eye, the uneasy twitch of a sinewy finger, would indicate Phelps is awake.

Awake? cries Phelps, having bobbed on the sea till eight at night, having rushed empty-handed to find out Snead. Awake? It mesmerised me!

For a second day Phelps takes Snead's boat; he clambers down to the creased shoreline, and shunts the bark out into the sea. The eery enchantment of dawn hangs over shapeless hills like a shroud. A light steady rain is shaken unseen from the measureless depths of the skies. A piercing breeze comes pinching the coast, hurrying pockets of mist. Phelps whistles as he pulls at the oars, rounding the point to the sea.

The anchor stamps the water. Phelps claps his hands at the cold; he licks the raindrops from his beard, braces himself in the slow-sighing boat, and sits.

The morning darkens. A film of fog draws in from the sea, closing around the motionless man, hugging him close to the cliff. Somewhere in time Phelps stands; he repositions the boat, he bites on a biscuit, he renews the bait on his hook. Then he sits again.

By the boathouse lanterns Phelps steers his vessel safely back to the shore. The wind whips round him as he berths the boat, as he finds his feet on the quay.

Snead. Snead in the shadow of fading embers, hunched in a stained yellow nook of the pub, trawling plump fingers through his wind-shocked beard, uncomfortably drinking alone. For the last two days Snead has swapped with Phelps – he has felt the salt, the throb of the engine, the roll of the boat, and the six-hook lines which he spins from the stern of a fishing smack as he's trawled in the open sea. The boat he has borrowed has been alive with convulsing shapes of mackerel, slapping their heads and tails on the deck, dancing contortions till glue-eyed death. Just once or twice he has raised his eyes, he has dared to look at his own proud craft, cradled in the calm of the cliff and captained by Phelps, in static pursuit of the bass.

Wild and wet as the third day breaks, Phelps' boat is on the sea as the grey surging mass meets dawn. The cliff the colour of fury, black breakers slapping against its scalp, Phelps rides out the hateful day, with a line laid low in the restless sea, in the rage of the estuary.

As dusk rolls in, the day regains its noble poise and smiles along the stretch of coast, caressing the ocean to rest. From the cliff, Snead looks down at the hungry man in the drifting boat, intent and absorbed, in the narrow waters, unmoving, just watching his line.

Snead discovers from Phelps' wife how bad the affliction is. He is gone in the morning before she wakes, and returns wet and hungry, in time for bed. In his sleep he mutters of fish. She wouldn't mind, she confides in Snead, if only Phelps would bring one home. But she has never seen a bass, and now she thinks she never will. Tomorrow they must leave.

And what then, she demands of Snead, if there is still no bass in sight? Will Phelps continue as he has – talking, dreaming, living bass – and sell his soul to fish? Will he reject his worldly goods – his wife, his kids, his job, his home – and stay here bobbing on the sea until he catches one? How could he be so desperately boring, sitting there day after day on his own, watching the line without ever moving, hoping a fish is foolish enough to take a spontaneous swipe?

Snead. Snead in the pub, when in walks Phelps. Phelps who has been at sea all day. All day and still no bass. No bass, but still one last attempt. Attempting a smile, Snead toys with the pitcher of beer in his hands. His hands steer meaning back to Phelps. Phelps, take my boat, and with it take me! Is there not room for two?

Not room for two. Mrs Phelps endures an account of Phelps' inglorious day; she serves supper, goes to bed, dreams not of the bass, wakes up without Phelps, and phones Snead's home to discover from Mrs Snead that Snead is out – he is hiding on the cliff, watching Phelps, who in turn is watching his line. She has lunch, does the packing, cooks supper, and hoovers; she lies on the sofa with a foot in the air, reading a book, and waiting for Phelps.

Phelps comes home, but late, and alone. His supper and his side of the bed are both cold.

Daybreak. Snead casts a curious eye at the jetty. His boat is there on its mooring. Then Phelps has gone. Gone has Phelps. Phelps. Gone.

Over a passive sea a gull floats, wings akimbo, crying. Patches of cloud glide over the fields; the estuary curls, curvaceous and pregnant, out towards a waiting sea. The brown-red, ponderous cliff stands proud. It glows like a welcoming fire.

Squinting through the glare of the morning, Snead finds himself unusually nervous as he walks to his boat to fish for bass.

Time

'What is a minute?'

'A minute is sixty seconds.'

'What is a second?'

'It depends. A second is 'one monkey'. When you are older and you can say 'monkey' quickly, a second is more like 'one elephant'.'

'So seconds get bigger?'

'No, seconds stay the same. You get bigger. Seconds aren't big or small. Seconds are long.'

'How long?'

'About *that* long.'

'That's not long.'

'No. But when you put them together they are long.'

'How long?'

'Very long, if you have enough of them.'

'How many seconds are enough?'

'Enough for what?'

'Enough to be long.'

'Well, that depends. Sixty seconds is a minute, and sixty minutes is an hour. And an hour can be a very long time. An hour is sitting in the car and driving for fifty miles…'

'That's long. That's ever so long…'

'Or watching ten cartoons, or…'

'That's not long. Hey! That's not long!'

'Yes, it is. It's still an hour.'

'It's not a long hour.'

'Well it might not seem as long, but it is as long. It's still sixty minutes.'

'I think car hours are long and cartoon hours are short.'

'That's because time goes faster when you are enjoying yourself.'

'That's not fair! I wish it was always the same.'

'It is the same.'

'You said it goes faster when you're having fun.'

'It seems to go faster, though in fact it actually goes just the same.'

'That doesn't make sense, if sometimes it goes faster and sometimes slower, but really it's all the same.'

'That's the way it is. Something called relativity.'

'O…! Why do we have time?'

'So we can tell the beginning from the end, and how long there is in between. It helps us to plan things. When to get up, when to have lunch, and when to go to bed. It lets me know how old you are.'

'You know how old I am! You don't need to be told!'

'Well, we need it for other things too. To make sense of days and weeks and months and years. Without time we wouldn't know where we were. We wouldn't know what year it was.'

'You could guess…'

'Yes, we could guess, but we wouldn't know.'

'And you could tell what month it was by what the weather was like, and if there were leaves on the trees, and that sort of thing.'

'Yes, we could, but we wouldn't know.'

'And what time of day it was by if it was light or dark, or where the sun was in the sky.'

'Maybe.'

'And lunchtime would be when you're hungry.'

'That's true. But we wouldn't know for sure.'

'Why would we want to?'

'Because we would. We need to know when things are, and how long they take.'

'Why? What's the point when some things take longer than others?'

'Well, imagine what life without time would be like. Friends wouldn't know when to come and play. We wouldn't know when to go on holiday. I wouldn't know when to give you your pocket money. Just imagine that…!'

'So what did we do before time began?'

'I'm sorry?'

'What did people do before time started?'

'It didn't start. It's always existed. Only we haven't always measured it.'

'What did we do before then?'

'I guess we used to do what you want to do now. It's quite likely that we've always been aware of the concept of time, only we haven't always had a way to measure it. We grow up sensing that when things come to an end they go into the past. And sensing that other things will happen at some point in the future, even though we don't know when. Time goes in a line that way, and it goes round and round as well. There is day and then night, and that night is followed by another day. Even the earliest people worked that out for themselves. They knew that when leaves fell off the trees the spring would return in a while. They knew that the natural cycle repeats. They probably ate when they were hungry, and had a bath when it all got a bit too smelly for comfort. So I suppose they had their own way of time-keeping, even before someone came up with the bright idea of dividing it into seconds and minutes and months and years.'

'How can seconds and stuff just be an idea?'

'Well, because that's all they really are. They're things we've invented to help us make sense of what we mean when we talk about time. They're not actually time itself. If we decided to do away with minutes and talked about sixty frankfurters in an hour it wouldn't make any difference. If we decided to have a hundred minutes in an hour, or in fact if we decided to do away with minutes altogether, time would be just the same, and continue in much the same way. It's the way we measure it that would change, that's all.'

'So time's been around forever?'

'Yup.'

'And when does it stop?'

'Never.'

'Not even when you die?'

'It won't stop for other people, even if it might for you.'

'So it goes on forever?'

'Yup, it goes on for eternity. In fact, eternity is what we say when we talk about things that exist beyond time.'

'And how far through eternity are we?'

'Who knows? Time has no beginning and no ending, so we can't even be somewhere in the middle. We're just sort of here. In a fraction of eternity.'

'O.'

'In fact, if you think about it, we're always here, because it's always now. Only this now isn't the same as that one…'

'Which one?'

'The one that happened a couple of frankfurters ago.'

'Dad?'

'Yes, Jessie.'

'How long is this now going to last?'

'Which now?'

'That now.'

'I'm not sure. It would be nice to think that if we waited for long enough it might come round again, and then we could measure it.'

'Dad?'

'Yes, Jessie.'

'I hope the next one's going to last a bit longer. Do you think it will?'

'Who knows? It might just last forever...'

The Fisherman's Tale

I suppose it all came about as a result of that night, several weeks ago, when I announced that I wished I was dead.

It hadn't been a particularly memorable day. We were having dinner, and Harry had just left the room with the dishes when, casting a cursory eye over the wizened company before me, it occurred to me how utterly pointless life was. There we sat, five proud monuments to time, at that feast – the sole event of interest in our long, somnambulant days – in complete silence. All semblance of life had gone with Harry. Those who remained were living a lie, living a dream, living on something that wasn't our own. We were moribund; we were waiting for death; it stood but a hair's breadth away.

In truth, I was sick to the teeth with them all. I was fed up with Priscilla and her constant complaints about her heart and her swollen ankles. I was tired of watching TV with Zak merely so I could change the channels, since the old sod couldn't do it himself. I was tired of Charles – the only rational person amongst them – telling us tedious tales from the past, from his former life as a dentist. And yes, I was tired of Prue; of Prue, whom Nature, the Fates, or some force had left to spin her dwindling thread till she had come to the age of ninety-two. Prue, who dribbled her life away. On her clothes, on the carpet, on the person beside her – always, forever dribbling.

They revolted me. All four of them. All four mumbling, bumbling, fumbling old fools who were sat around the table; and I the one who put them up, the one who had to live with them. It was murder. Each was no more than a bag of bones, spoiled by ailments, more dead than alive. And combined, we made up a mausoleum to our semi-departed selves. Our life together was one long day, one continuous non-event, identical to the last. We were detached from reality; divorced from vitality. We were living a fabricated existence, a stream of inconsequent weeks and months that comprised a single perpetual day – a day devoid of any sensation, incapable of provoking response. The only break from its chronic inertia had to be brought by our death.

Ah death! How sweet it must be. How enthralling for those who entered its snare, or for those who witnessed its coming and passing as it seized the one to their side. But for us there was no consolation. Something or someone was torturing us, elongating our vacuous lives, laughing at us and our morbid desire, refusing stem the flow of our torpor or cut the thread which yet held us to life.

So I had stood up and declared that I wished I was dead.

That is not to say, of course, that I wanted to die. I was simply rehearsing its relative merits, depicting a sensible substitute to our hollow insensible lives. A position the others should have applauded had they opened their eyes to its truth.

But they did not. My outburst was met by inevitable silence. The company clumped and clawed at their food, deaf to what I had said.

That, at least, is how I perceived it. Though, the next day, as Harry laid out the supper in front of his semi-comatose charges, I noticed that mine was obviously different.

'Why?!'

Every person around the table stopped in the midst of their mindless motions, and looked up. Surprised, perhaps, I was still awake, or that from the atrophy of my brain I had managed to summon a word.

'Why?!' I repeated.
'Why what?' Harry inquired.
'Mine's different…'

Harry, who knows everything that needs to be known, who cannot flinch in the face of the truth – even when Prue is dribbling on him – explained that he wished to avoid confusion.

'What the hell do you mean?!'
'Yours is different, Sir.'
'I can see it is different. I want to know why.'
'Because of what you said last night.'
'What did I say? Tell me! What do you think I said?!'

Harry, dismayed by the onset of my apparent dementia, felt obliged to enlighten me further – 'Your boeuf bourguignon is poisoned, Sir.'

Now, I would hope from all I have said thus far it is clear that I am the only one of these people who can make any claim to be sane. The exception being Harry, my man. So for him to have uttered such a statement caused me no little concern.

I looked towards my wrinkled companions in the hope of gaining edification in the light of Harry's absurdity, though that exercise itself was absurd. Instead, I addressed him once more.

'Poisoned, Harry?'
'That is correct, Sir.'
'O, dear god!'

In spite of myself, my exasperation was overwhelmed by the weight of lethargy. I felt no urge to determine the truth of such a preposterous lie. These scarecrows had neither the wit nor the will to execute a practical venture as complex as poisoning my meal. It was equally inconceivable that Cook should have dished up her revenge, or that Harry should derelict his duty. Any explanation would be more absurd than the assertion that had preceded it, and I refused to let it have breath.

Instead, I grasped the plate with both hands and threw it forcefully to the floor – quite at a loss for another gesture that would satisfy my rage.

Curiously, as the plate splintered in fragments before me, a spontaneous and unprompted sensation arose: a regenerative force, a powerful resurgence of something long dormant – quiescent so long that it took me some time to understand what it was. Though in that moment there could be no doubting. I had been struck by emotion, feeling, passion. Something akin to being alive.

Something had happened. I had done something – something dynamic and real. Exhilaration was stealing within me, prompting me to project my napkin, my cutlery and even my wine glass after the steaming dish of food. Prompting me to utter a scream at witnessing the lovely mess strewn randomly on the floor. I might have gone further still, I might have rekindled my relish for life, I might have reaffirmed my existence, if I hadn't have stopped and looked at my guests, if I hadn't have seen their impassive attention already returned to their own sorry dishes, and to the solid stagnancy of their lives.

Damn them! In defiance, I rose and stomped from the room.

When I returned, some five minutes later, and placed my ear against the keyhole, all I could hear was their cutlery clinking, the occasional crash as things were knocked over, and perhaps – within the most resonant lulls – even the sound of Prue's dribbling.

Nothing had changed after all.

Later that night, whether taking a chill from my earlier exertions, or, like a child, in need of the comfort of light and warmth, I summoned Harry and instructed him to light the fire within the great hall, and to make up my bed before it. The others had all retired to their rooms; the house was sombre and still. When Harry had finished I went downstairs and basked in the easy glow of the fire, tracing shadows of monstrous proportion that flickered against the oak-paneled walls, and musing over their counterparts framed in the seething embers and flames.

There I must have fallen asleep. The fire, too, did not sustain its vigil, for it was no more than a pile of ash when I was awakened from uneasy slumber in the very dead of the night.

I cannot say what might have disturbed me. I suppose it may have been a nightmare, for I was bathed in sweat, though my throat was dry. I rose and felt my way through the shadow towards the kitchen to fetch a drink.

That wake was as cryptic as my dream, for as I retraced my steps to the hall I discerned a vision of Prue in the darkness, dressed as would befit a dream in her dead husband's ancient safari gear, with his shotgun clasped in her hands.

This detail in particular suggested to me it might be a dream, for I knew she had an aversion to guns, and never accompanied her dead husband on shooting parties to game reserves save when a certain Colonel Mathieson was included as one of the group.

I thought it prudent I should linger awhile, undetected in the shadows, as I watched the apparition approach my bed and halt at its foot, before discharging both of the barrels into the heap of sheets and blankets without the slightest of hesitation. Then the phantom smiled its sympathy; it stepped back and uttered the soothing words – 'There, there, my angel. All's better now.'

An extraordinary living dream it was. Though the event, the detail, the blasts themselves, were all too vivid, too real, too loud to be creations of my mind. I called out to Prue to confirm my suspicions. The antiquated creature turned around towards the sound, her skeletal fingers rearming the piece with remarkable deftness and speed. Then she raised and aimed the instrument in the vague direction of my voice, where she must have supposed me to be.

In that very same moment, with some agitation, the reality of my predicament impressed itself upon me. A feeling that was reinforced when an Ottoman vase not far from my shoulder shattered under the force of the shot, while the remaining discharge passed over my head and embedded itself in the oak-cladded walls.

Knowing this was no longer a dream, Prue's actions confirmed my deep-set suspicion that the poor girl was completely insane.

This thought aside, I had half a mind to confront the old dear, when I remembered the same Colonel Mathieson once saying that Prue had proven a marvelous shot when he took her out for instruction alone. Not wanting to put this claim to the test at the expense of my own person – in case it turned out to be true – I decided to loiter under cover of shadow until her cartridges were all spent, or she expired beneath the weight of the gun. I crept through the darkness till I was positioned directly behind where the barrels were pointing. Then I watched her as she peered through the gloom, haphazardly aiming at objects and shadows, hearing the charges puncture the pitch, then cocking her head and crying aloud – 'Are you still with us, Martin?'

This performance was repeated for a full five minutes, during which I noted several antiques would need to be scratched from my will. Finally, Prue exhausted her rounds; then – having failed to force a groan from the dark – she let the weapon slip from her hands, and stood mute and motionless, framed in the crust of the dying ember, fragile and small, and touchingly helpless.

I spared her the pain of further shame by coming forward and taking her shoulders, whispering as gently as I was able – 'Don't worry, Prue. I'll get your pills.'

It was with a last gasp of wounded pride that she shrieked – 'Sod the bloody pills!' I confess this took me a little aback. Nevertheless, I mounted the stairs to go to my room and fetch my own tablets – hearing, as I did so, the sound of her scrabbling to snatch up the gun, and the aimless clicking of hammers on air in the empty chambers behind me.

What a delightful adventure! When was the last time something had happened – something, anything out of the usual – to shake us from our malaise?! Such thoughts, I am sure, would have busied my mind had I not been so concerned about Prue, and the demons that had possessed her. As it was, I was wholly preoccupied with the task of finding some pills. I went to my room and sought out the medicine on top of my bedside drawers. I was turning back to go downstairs, when Zak appeared at the door in his wheelchair. He was dressed in a pair of bright green pyjamas, with a large axe laid in his lap. He spun his way towards me swiftly.

'Zak, my dear chap' I began, 'did you hear all that noise? Prue's had a hell of a turn…'
'Be quiet, little man! Dying time's here.'

Zak always liked to make an entrance. He had a good sense of humour too. This, though, wasn't the time for jesting. I tried to tell him, but to no avail.

Zak hurtled towards me at speed, attempting to trap me against the wall. And, as his hands inevitably moved from the wheels to the mighty truncheon he carried, I sensed that the man had spoken in earnest, and retreated onto the balcony.

Zak determinedly followed behind me, blocking all means of escape. As ill luck would have it, the terrace was small. It is said that the mason had been beheaded on the instruction of Queen Anne for failing to follow the architect's drawings. I think it had something to do with the weight, and the mason's fear that the specifications would lead to the structure collapsing entirely – perhaps even with his monarch still on it. Such is the price some people pay for the thoughtfulness they bestow.

I digress.

Zak wheeled himself onto the balcony and, after several painful attempts, managed to rise from his chair. He was even able to raise the axe-head high above his own. I was tempted to congratulate him on this feat, though I feared he may not have gone to such lengths merely to show his prowess.

'Zak…' I entreated, but to no effect. Already he was wielding the weapon; he was shuffling forwards towards me.

'Zak…' The heavy instrument hung in the air, before crashing down and embedding itself in the low wooden railing beside me.

Zak cursed.

'Really, old chap! You've been watching too many of your films, haven't you?' I remonstrated.

He cursed again, his face visibly crimsoning in the early blushes of dawn. He was grumbling most unreasonably too, and refusing any offer of help I might give him to tug the axe free.

'Never mind' I said, 'I'll go and get a saw, and we'll have the thing out in a jiffy.'

As I slipped past him however, a dilemma presented itself. Should I first find Zak's saw, or give Prue her pills? Which of them needed it most? Caught in two minds I turned towards Zak, wanting to seek his advice.

At that precise moment, Zak must have exerted the exact ounce of effort required to release the axe from the rail, for the steel came loose and was suddenly free. It came loose so cleanly it sprung in the air, all the way over his head. And it didn't stop there. The force of motion that came from Zak was transferred from him to the axe's head, and being of a substantial weight it continued in its arching flight, having nothing to stand in its way. Zak, taken aback, was either too slow or too obstinate to let the handle slide from his grasp. So, when the steel went over the balcony, Zak did too – pulled precipitously, accelerating in a perfect arc, as a fisherman might be hauled overboard when a mighty shark takes hold of his hook – before I was able to come to his aid.

First, Zak was there. Then he was not.

I rushed to the edge of the balcony. I looked out into the grey pool of dawn; I called out over the chill morning air – 'Zak! Zak!' – hearing my cry dissolve on the wind, hearing its echo melt in my ears.

Then I saw him.

Zak was… Zak was… dead. I couldn't doubt it, seeing him laid on a fresh bed of earth, a foot to the right of a rhododendron flush in the full bloom of flower.

I descended the stairs in haste, and made for the door which led to the garden. As I passed the hall I caught sight of Prue, collapsed in front of the fire. Finding the pills were still in my hand I decided I ought to go to her first, and then to attend to Zak.

I knelt down beside her; I lifted her small and insensible body; I carried her up the stairs to her room; I laid her out on her bed. I had hardly had time to force some pills down her throat before she stirred from her stupor. She sat up, and tentatively asked where she was. I was loath to tell her of Zak's escapade, so I quietened her down as best I was able. I told her to lie back and sleep.

'Thank you. Thank you', she murmured, seeming oblivious of all that had happened, resting her infant hands on my shoulders with the touch of a midnight child.

'Go to sleep, my dear' I soothed, 'I'll see you later.' And I placed the rest of the pills by her bed before creeping out of her room.

As the door was opening, as the dusky light from emerging day spilt into the darkened room, I heard a gurgle behind me. Turning, I saw the sleep-laden body neither sitting nor lying, locked in a sudden, unnatural posture – her palms on her cheeks; her fingers pressed on the pulse of her temples; her fierce little eyes on the bottle of pills.

'These… these pills… they're yours.'

'Yes. They're just the same as yours. Sleeping stuff.'

'No, no! They are *yours*. You didn't give me *yours*, did you, Martin?'

'Of course I did, Prue. I don't know where you keep your own.'

'But you can't give me these! You can't give them to me!'

'Why ever not?'

'Because I poisoned them! I poisoned them!'

'_'

'No! No! You bloody man! You bastard!'

And for the first time in my life I think I knew how the stonemason felt when he felt the wrath of Queen Anne.

Prue was spitting on the counterpane, attempting to make herself sick. And she was dribbling as much as she could. Yet all her efforts were futile. The dose she had delivered was so strong that she lay in my arms for less than ten minutes, struggling to keep her body alive. Then, suddenly, she gave up her soul to that unknown world which awaits us all, and I was left holding a fragile sack of tortured flesh and brittle bones, rocking it gently on my knees in the slack and tardy pre-dawn dusk, feeling its life no more.

Somewhere, on some distant shore, I swore as I sat in that curious silence, there, all alone, I could hear the heart-strings of Colonel Mathieson rend and snap for a final time. Dismissed for conduct unbecoming, a disgrace to the Highlander's uniform, yet gallant and true to her still. Loving in hopeless expectation, right to this very point.

Poor Prue!

But not long after – just as the tentative rays of dawn were searching into the tomb of Prue's room – I was overcome by a different emotion. Prue's pills, the Zak attack, and that episode with the poisoned food, led me to the certain conclusion that a conspiracy had been hatched against me, with the aim of seeing me dead.

All the occupants of my house were in some way involved in this treason. They had to be, for the poisoning had been openly stated to all. And since that was indisputable, I knew that I had misjudged them. There must have been within them all – in Prue and Zak, in Priscilla and Charles – a purpose, a reason to live, a desire: strong enough to tempt them to action, to steel their hearts so they might prevail. That thought alone aroused more envy than any outrage I felt.

And then another thought. Both Prue and Zak had attempted to kill me, and in doing so they had died. Priscilla and Charles were yet alive; surely they would still try.

Before they had a chance to wake, I rose and locked myself in my room.

Prue and Zak had both died. They had gone to a different realm – an uncertain world but a welcome one, if only because it signaled a change. Some respite from this lethargy. Though I couldn't be happy they had died, in dying I was happy for them. Happy they had moved on elsewhere, to somewhere different and new.

Yet what aberration had shaken their souls to be roused to a semblance of life? What had focused their energies with such vehemence, squarely on me?

It was then I remembered what I had said only the night before. They had, in good faith – no more and no less – taken me literally, at my word. They were acting under a dreadful illusion that by killing me they were able to help me.

O, the difference between wishing and wanting to die! Between sentiment and content!

They had determined I wanted to die, and had decided amongst themselves how best to execute the deed. With such insistence that the matter of when, or where, or even how it came were forced on me, against my will, out of compassion or out of desire to fulfil my latest request. Now, it appeared, they would stop at nothing until my wish had come true.

I went back to bed and tried to sleep, in the hope that sleep would smooth it away in the gentle deceit of my dreams. But it didn't. I sat in bed and scanned my room as though it were a hostile land, with an ambush laid in every nook. At least my door was not besieged; a ladder had not scaled my walls. Yet make no mistake, this was war. A siege that would surely end in death. A desperate struggle I had brought on myself by my vain and foolhardy words.

I had brought it all upon myself. My only choice was to see it through.

I went to the window. Zak's broken body had been removed, the axe had gone and the soil was raked into a smooth fine tilth. But in the yard there were two carpets, rolled and dense, beyond what seemed their natural bulk.

Harry had performed his duty with the same application, the same intent, as he always brought to his role. Though perhaps he was party to murder too. After all, he was privy to all the madness that went on in this house. No, Harry was Harry, the perfect man. Loyal, impartial to the end. I could have no doubt he was true. He may have served me poisoned food, but that was his job, to serve. Much as now, with the rolled-up rugs, he disposed of what we did not need. He prepared the ground and he cleared away. He witnessed all without casting judgement. But, foremost, he acted for me.

Rain creased down. The heavens rumbled, and the air was close. The thunder came spontaneously, like a petulant child, whilst the firmament, caught in the cast of a summer's day, held itself aloof and serene, removed from the closeness, the fire and the lightning, spitting and splitting the humid air.

And no wind.

It was early evening. The thunder sulked, lurking hatred deep in the throat of ponderous clouds, smitten by its own sheer strength and potency. Now the parched soil lay in wait of the beneficence of soothing rain to quench its thirst and drown its grief, to wash the stain away. A single raindrop presaged all, pressed against my windowpane. And then, exquisite downpour. Shafts of brilliance; translucent threads of light. A deluge, biting as it fell, thick with the stick and smell of summer, slanting through the heavy air, discharging, creating wind as it fell. Then straight it came, in vertical lines, piercing the earth with insistent spears – enriching, dissolving, burning.

I looked out onto the bloated moat. I was a prisoner within my own home. My domain extended as far as my door. My single choice was whether I dared to pull at its handle and look beyond. To enter again the great unknown: my house which I thought I knew so well. To stay in my room amounted to death, for the living unseen are seen as if dead. Though to trespass further meant entering a world where everyone wanted me dead.

It was a quarter to nine. The house was quiet. It was wrapped in stillness; a fixed, firm silence of stern intent. More threatening than if my assailants were wrenching the door apart from its frame, or tearing the shutters away from their hinges, or ripping the roof from the face of the walls, rafter by rafter, tile by tile.

The sky had grown a darker shade; the windows were open to the night. The thunder had cleared its throat and slept; a sheet of rain continued to fall as a curtain of light, blindly, unseen. Only random droplets of water pierced the pane which slid before me, landing on my balcony at discord with the rest.

I turned from the purple sky and the fluid rain, to the lonely lament of a single bulb which hung from the ceiling rose in my room. The filament was buzzing and twitching, in spasms, as if the current that brought it life was weakening, on the point of failure, preparing to cast me into the dark.

And I knew in my heart that though much of the world was hidden from me, the one thing I did not want right then was to find myself alone in the dark.

The next morning I summoned Harry. There were so many questions I wanted to ask him, so many questions that begged a reply – the bodies, the food, the others, himself. Yet when he arrived, with a tray full of breakfast, assuming an air of the utmost indifference, I realised that foraging into the truth would only be met with silence. Harry knew all that there was to be known, but he kept his confidence close.

He laid the tray beside my bed whilst I stood by the window, watching his movement, clutching a chair-leg behind my back. He went about his usual duties without the slightest hesitation, having no doubt I held a weapon, having no doubt I would not strike. Such is the comfort of knowing oneself to be utterly indispensable. He did not need to persuade himself; he knew it came with the job.

'Is the food poisoned?'
'No, Sir.'

Instinctively I believed him. Harry is unable to lie.

As if hearing my thoughts, he glanced up. He almost met with my eyes.

'Would you like me to taste it, Sir?'

I waved him away with my one free arm; and Harry, who had ascertained the object hidden behind my back – without need to consult the tables and chairs – put forward a further proposal –

'Would you like me to mend your chair, Sir?'

I hesitated for a moment. To have clung onto the chair-leg obstinately would have given him a moral victory, yet to have yielded the object up to him would lead to an actual one. Harry knew it, and in knowing it so, he knew he exceeded his bounds.

'Harry...' He looked up dutifully, anticipating a reprimand; or maybe a shameful and intimate secret he could take to his breast and treasure forever –

'... Piss off!' The trace of a smile appeared and was gone. And so was he, in that instant. Across the floor, towards the door, out into the passage, and then no more. The man was beyond reproach.

That afternoon I unlocked my door. I sat on the bed and patiently waited for someone to enter my room. I had the chair-leg close to hand, persuading myself it ensured a fair contest when mortal combat ensued. I reckoned we would be squarely matched if Charles was revealed my adversary, and that I would be clear favourite if Priscilla entered the fray.

I did the same the following day, and then again the next. The day after that I went so far as to leave my door ajar. I even sat at the roll-top desk, pretending to busy myself in my work, presenting myself side on.

But they did not come. They must have been waiting; they must have hatched a plan of their own. One that involved me being elsewhere – not here, in the quiet of my room.

It was inquisitiveness that lured me downstairs, a few days later: my baton clasped tight in my fist to my side, hugging the walls and peering round corners, checking the doors for explosive devices, before creeping into the shade of the garden by the wrought-iron table and chairs.

It was almost eleven; it was time for coffee. I was sure their routine hadn't changed. Sure enough, before very long, Priscilla arrived, walking in that curious fashion which involves moving sideways rather than forwards – her left foot crossing over her right, and her right then creeping under her left.

Seeing her so – so quite decrepit – I could almost believe she was ignorant of Zak and Prue and their whole desperate plot. She was ignorant and innocent, caught in the snare of early dementia, blissfully unaware of intrigue. This feeling grew as she made me out from beneath the shadow of foliage, as she wished me a bright and brisk good morning, much as she always had.

A short while later Charles arrived, seeming equally nonchalant. He sat down in his usual chair with a grunt of a greeting into the bush where I had concealed myself. Then he proceeded to open a beer, and attack the crossword without reference to the clues: filling the squares with words such as 'bullshit' and 'cockscomb' until the grid was complete.

Given the level of passive aggression I took courage and seated myself beside them, pretending to busy myself in a book, secreting my chair-leg under the table, till Harry came out with the coffee and cake.

I spent the whole of the day with them. All that week, and then into the next. Ostensibly calm though constantly vigilant, awaiting a sudden attack.

Then, one evening, having bid them goodnight and retired to the door, having hidden behind it and listened attentively, I chanced upon this exchange –

'When shall we do it?'

'Do what?'

'When shall we kill him?'

'Who?'

'Him.'

'Who?'

'Martin, of course.'

'Are we still trying to kill him?'

'That's the idea, isn't it?'

'Is it? Yes, I suppose that it is.'

'—'

'Why did we want to kill him?'

'I can't remember exactly. Can you?'

'—'

'I remember the others tried…'

'Tried what?'

'Tried to kill him.'

'Did they? Which others?'

'The other people who used to live here.'

'Why?'

'I don't know why they used to live here. They just did.'

'No, why did they try to kill him?'

'Kill who?'

'Kill whatever-he's-called.'

'I'm not sure. That was what I was just saying.'

'Where are the others anyway?'

'Who?'

'The ones that used to live here. The one in the wheelchair.'

'I can't remember a wheelchair.'

'No, nor can I. Perhaps it was crutches.'

'—'

'—'

'He did say he wanted to die.'

'Who?'

'Martin.'

'Well let him die if he wants to.'

'Shouldn't we try to help him?'

'I suppose we could try. What should we do?'

'There are so many ways it's hard to choose.'

'Don't you think he'll die on his own?'

'On his own?'

'Most people do.'

'But it could take forever, poor chap.'

'Yes, poor chap. A horrible dilemma.'

'So let's help him, shall we?'

'Absolutely. What are we going to do again?'

'We're going to kill the old bugger.'

'Now? After supper? I'm a bit tired now. Couldn't we do it in the morning?'

'Yes. Yes. Whenever you want. You just say when you're ready.'

'_'

'_'

'Killing isn't the same as dying though.'

'Well, it leads to the same result.'

'It's not actually the same, you know. Everyone dies, but they're not all killed.'

'This is a mercy killing. We're helping him to die, that's all. He asked for it.'

'Why's he asking for it?'

'He's not asking for it, he asked for it. He actually asked us to kill him.'

'Did he? What a silly man.'

'Silly yes. But rich. Lucky he's got friends like us, who will stick with him through thick and thin.'

'_'

'_'

'Did you like him?'

'Who?'

'The rich guy you were talking about.'

'Who, Martin?'

'Yes.'

'What do you mean, did I like him?'

'Well, did you? I liked him. At least, I thought he was all right.'

'But he's not dead.'

'I thought you said he was.'

'No, I said we were going to kill him.'

'O.'

'Then he'll be dead.'

'Ah.'

'And then we can have this conversation.'

'That's nice. Something to look forward to.'

'Quite.'

'_'

'_'

'Though, if we don't do anything, maybe he'll do it himself. If he really wants to.'

'He may do. I'm not sure we can rely on him to do it, that's all.'

'Don't you think…?'

'No. He's a ditherer. He's never had a real job in his life, and he probably never will. We need to give him a push.'

'Are we going to push him over? Do you think that will kill him?'

'It might, yes. Or we might try something more reliable.'

'Why don't we tell him to get on with it if he really wants to do it?'

'He hates being told what to do.'

'If we asked him kindly…'

'Certainly not. Firm persuasion is needed if we want him to do it himself. We need to get it into his head that killing himself is the right thing to do. He's a stubborn bugger, and that's going to take lots of effort. It will be easier to kill him ourselves.'

'Poor man. He must be tired of life if he wants to die. But I don't think trying to kill him will help. If he's afraid of being killed he'll avoid us, he'll do all he can to stay alive. He'll have found a reason to live. And that's not what anyone wants. So if you stop trying to kill him he won't feel afraid. Remove the threat and things will return to the way they were. After a while he'll get bored. When he's bored enough he'll get tired of living. And then there's a chance he'll give it a go. He'll want to die to compare it to living. Just for the sake of a change. Then, when he's dead, he'll come to see that life wasn't dull after all. Don't you think?'

'No, Charles. He needs us to give him a helping hand.'

I had heard enough, and crept back up to my room. Once more on my own I felt safe. Safe because it was clear to me they had yet to determine whether to kill me, and yet to decide on the means.

What startled me more was not what was said, but that they had spoken at all. More words were exchanged in that last half an hour than had been shared in a year. Both were engaged and enthused by the moment, excited by something that stirred in their being: the prospect of seeing me dead. They had persuaded themselves that sooner or later, for good or for worse, by my hand or theirs, I would die. And that expectation gave them a hunger, a purpose, a focus. What I had said had roused them to life – as much as it had rekindled my own.

In the days that followed our different desires grew more intense and acute. The pursuit became a preoccupation, an obsession that captured us all. We may have returned to our old routine, yet now we had something to live for. Relentlessly and continuously they prompted me with hints and suggestions, they passed me sharp objects, they told me stories that might induce me to die. For my part, too, I sulked and swore, I threatened violence on myself – enough, I hoped, to give them hope that I would do what they would do were I not bold enough to do it.

I savoured their immense delusion; though I feared it could not last, I didn't know how it would end. I strove to strike a precious balance, feeding them sufficient scraps to stop them killing me themselves because I promised that myself, although I found the grounds to stay the execution day by day. And so a week passed by. Within a clear and shallow pool I dropped my baited hook, I drew it teasingly in idle circles round the snouts of woken fish which swam with increased urgency around the thing of their desire, the single object of allure.

The more we waited and we watched, the more obsessive we became. The harder each one tried. Each one eager for that moment: wanting the accomplishment on which the three of us depended; in denial of the truth of emptiness which lined its wake.

Knowing that at some point he or she or I would slip – making a mistake from which there could be no escape.

Nothing can endure forever, no matter how each part is played. For pressure builds on all the actors: each determined to outshine, each restless till their goal is reached. And so it proved with them.

For me the goal was not to die; for them, to shepherd me to death. And that is where the contest failed. For it is easier to live than to coerce a soul to die. My role demanded less than theirs; all I had to do was wait. Charles seemed content with their approach; he seemed to think that in the end the end they sought would come about. But his accomplice lacked restraint; Priscilla showed no clemency. Impatience steered her speech and deeds, by degrees the more outlandish, till she reached a stage at which she could no longer sit and wait.

So it was that one fine dusk we sat for dinner in the garden, watching the declining day, discussing ways by which to die. Harry moved invisibly, clearing up the dregs of soup. Charles, well-fortified by ale, had nodded off while sitting upright, staring out of sightless eyes. Priscilla, waiting edgily for the next course of sirloin steak, made the mistake of fidgeting and touched upon her knife. Feeling the raw power of steel within her grasp, and glancing at its jagged blade, she snatched it up and stood and grimaced. Then, quite suddenly, she lunged towards me, stabbing at the air.

I had foreseen just such a move, and as she came at me I slid from where I sat and sought my shelter on the farther side of Charles, where Harry stood and stacked the bowls with admirable indifference.

Priscilla snarled.

We took two turns around the table at great pace, somehow avoiding waking Charles; while Harry skillfully maneuvered his supper tray towards the house – stopping, starting, pirouetting, as both of us brushed past. Then, for fear of giddiness, I stretched out straight into the open, making for the orchard and a clutch of apple trees. Glancing back I saw Priscilla, commendably still in pursuit despite the anguish of her ankles, forging a consistent path though safely far behind.

Three weeks had passed since Prue and Zak had made their failed attempts on me, and in that while Priscilla's patience had been worn beyond endurance. She could no longer wait for me to dither on the place and time; she had decided it herself. That time and place were now. That was how I figured it, gauged by her furious sideways charge, gauged by the frenzy of her screams demanding me to halt.

I had reached the trees and could have continued – perhaps as far as the local pub where I used to drink in those aimless days when Charles and I knew nothing else – had I not heard a noise behind me, tempting me to turn.

From behind me came a wretched cry, one full of anguish and of pain. Priscilla's ankles had worn out, and she was sprawling on the ground.

I arrived at her side at the same time as Harry, who carried a sponge and a bowl of warm water to mop first her brow then her feet. But once this was done it was clear from her breathing that the problem was less the feet than the heart. This brief exertion by Priscilla, the first for a decade or maybe longer, had been sufficient to overwhelm her, and she was struggling for life.

Charles was woken, yet however hard he looked into her mouth he could not determine the state of her heart. It was Harry who came again to the fore, Harry who knew what had to be done – Harry who always seems to know. He laid Priscilla onto her back, and attempted to resuscitate her.

For several minutes he knelt to her side, opening her airway, compressing her chest, watching for signs of her breath. Evening had come. The apple trees stood starkly around us, whispering a tuneless lament. Startled pools of lurching shadow stained the darkened earth.

I looked back at Harry; he was sitting on his haunches; his arms hung limp by his sides. And in that moment I knew for certain that Priscilla was with us no more.

So it was. Charles and I returned to the table. We had port and cheese, then a cup of coffee – just the two of us, in perfect silence – both that night and for the nights that followed, for as long as we both remained in the house, for as long as we lived there together.

From that moment on our relationship altered. Charles forged an unspoken contract with me, that though he wanted to see me die he would not try to harm me himself, and do as the others had done. Priscilla's death had influenced him, because he witnessed it for himself. Unlike the deaths of Prue and Zak, he had seen Priscilla's life drain from her, he had stared at the face of what lies beyond, and what he had seen had scared him.

We became increasingly close. He rarely wanted to leave my side. He clung to the hope he could press me to die; it became his purpose, his singular goal; as if unaware that however it ended, it was bound to end with regret.

And so it went on. The world closed around us; it stifled the need for actions or words. By willpower alone he urged me to die, and that inspired him to eke out existence, sustaining the span of his miserable life. We entered a new state of wretched survival, much as the one at the start of my tale, in which living meant nothing but staying alive, or wishing the other one dead.

Charles' life was lived for me; through me he kept himself alive. That may have been enough for him, yet I took nothing in return. Instead, he was my constant sore, my endless irritation. A bitter and unwelcome shadow, shielding me within the dark, far from the warmth and light of day. I knew he lacked the strength to kill. Knowing that, I feared my life would lose all meaning since its meaning was wrapped up in the fear of death. While Zak and Prue had been alive the threat had goaded me to live, to feel the life-force in my veins, inspiring me to come alive. But when they died that threat had waned, and with Priscilla it was dead. Charles wasn't an adversary. Persuasion lacked the force of threats, hints weren't translated into deeds. I feared the danger of relapse, of sliding into waking slumber, knowing there was no escape. I feared I would become like Charles. More barren still, more purposeless, for having nothing to achieve. Nothing more than Charles himself: this toothless torment, this decay, which grew and fed on me.

Then how was it to end?

I could do as they wanted of me. I could take my life, and in that act I could satisfy them all. But would it do so? Three of them were dead already. One remained, and with my death would he be more content? Charles may have wanted me to die, yet when I died then he would too, for having nothing left. He suffered as he watched me live; he suffered knowing I would die. All around him death stood proud, and mocked him with its certainty. The single point in which he lived was that which lay between both states: in which he coaxed me to the death I never quite attained. He clung to this obsessively – more than I dreamt of it myself, more than I meant for it to be. He sought into its very heart, and nestled in its core, its soul. In doing so he starved me of my own invention: stealing what was mine and spoiling it, corrupting it with twisted truths. Expecting me to stand and watch, to fuel it at my own expense.

And that was not the life for me.

And so, one night, I broke routine: I did not heed the dinner bell and follow it downstairs to feast. Instead, I stayed within my room. Presently, inevitably, there was a knock upon my door. It was Charles. So close he had become to me – this man who wanted me to die – that now he asked if I was well, if there was something I might need.

He found me sitting in my bed, dressed in my nightclothes, with a scarf tied round my neck, and hot water bottles to my sides.

'Are you ill?'
'Yes, I think I am.'
'I'll call a doctor. Wait!'

'Don't be silly. Come and sit down. I want to tell you a story. The story of the trout and the fisherman. Have you heard it before?'

'No I haven't, Martin. I think I should call a doctor first.'

'Never mind the doctor. There's nothing he can do.'

'What do you mean, nothing?'

'I mean what I've got will work itself through, whether he comes here or not. Anyway I don't like quacks. There was once an old man who spent his…'

'Not all medical professionals are quacks, you know.'

'All right, you can get a doctor. But let me finish my story first. It's only a short tale. Once upon a time there was an old…'

'This isn't a shaggy dog story, is it?'

'…old man, who spent all his day by the river at the end of his garden, fishing for a great fat trout which he knew was lying at the bottom of a pool. It lived in this pool, and it never moved…'

'How did he know it was there? Why didn't it move?'

'Because he could see it leaping about, almost as if it was taunting him. And because it didn't want to move. It was having fun playing the game.'

'Which game?'

'The game I am going to tell you about. Their obsession.'

'What obsession?'

'The fisherman was so obsessed by this fish that he spent the whole day angling, and then the whole night lying awake thinking of different strategies for how to capture the beast. He tied different flies, he read different books, he tried standing on different parts of the bank. Because no one ever came to his house, he had no distraction from his obsession. His life was tied to that of the fish. Yet despite all his efforts, at the end of each day he came away empty-handed. You see, the wily old trout knew the old man too well; he had fathomed all of his tricks. However good the fisherman was – and we must imagine he was the best – the trout was always more cunning than him. The fish didn't know what life would be like beyond the pool he had made his home, but he knew he was doing all right where he was. There was no incentive to move. And still the fisherman came each day; he was so determined he couldn't resist. What started once as a pleasurable pastime became a permanent occupation, a test of endurance, a battle of wills. Over the months they grew to learn all that could be learnt of the other. The old man knew how the fish would lie, where it ate, where it hid from the midday sun. And similarly the clever fat fish formed a clear impression of the old man. This wasn't a source of any great pleasure; it was a passion, a preoccupation – so much so that if one day one of them failed to return to the challenge, the other would surely have perished.'

'This is a shaggy dog story! Damn you, Martin, you do look bad.'

'So one day the fisherman comes down to the river and goes to one of his many places with one of his many devilish flies, and casts the line out over the trout. The fat trout knows it's the old man's line; it knows that it is much smarter than him. Yet, perhaps because it is tired of the game, perhaps because it wants to know what will happen when it takes the bait, or merely perhaps because of respect for the fisherman and his dogged persistence – for whatever reason grabs the trout – on this particular day it decides to swim over to the dangling hook and snatch it up in its mouth.'

'Don't tell me – the line breaks!'

'No, the line does not break. That is not how the story goes. The fisherman can't believe his luck. He reels the fish right into the bank, he pulls it out, knocks it on the head, stuffs it and mounts it, and goes to bed.'

'And that's it?'

'Yes, that is precisely it. You see, the fish is the whole of the old man's world. Every night he has only dreamt of the fish, so now he has nothing to fill his dreams. Nothing. The next day he wakes up, he puts on galoshes, and then he remembers it's already caught. So he takes down the case where the fat trout is mounted, and stares at the fish instead. But it doesn't look the same once it's dead. The challenge has gone, the excitement has vanished. What he holds in his hands could be any dead fish. He may have won the lengthy contest, but he is denied the victory. The fish has given in to him, and now the old man has no goal, no purpose, no desire. Think of it: all day and every day for months the old man has pursued his obsession, and now that obsession is ended. There are no more conquests, no other ambitions. His single aim has been achieved and has left him utterly drained. There is no enjoyment in anything else. His life has lost all meaning.'

'I bet the fish wasn't happy either.'

'You miss the point, you fool. The fish decided to give itself up. It actively determined its fate, even though that meant it would die. The fisherman, on the other hand, is left to wonder if he caught the fish by luck or by skill, or just because it had chosen to let itself be caught. He will never know; he is left not knowing. He is left in a barren world with no purpose, tormented by being alive. It is almost as if the canny fat trout knew how helpless the old man would be, and gave himself up for a laugh.'

'That's nonsense.'

'Why nonsense? The fish may die, but it makes that decision. The fisherman lives, but has nothing to live for. In fact he's worse off than if he were dead.'

'Great. Lovely story. Now let me get you the doctor.'

'You don't see, do you?'

'What?'

'You don't see the point of my story. You don't see what I am trying to say. I am the fish. I am the trout.'

'Gulp, gulp. Good for you. What are you talking about?'

'I am giving myself up to torment you.'

'Don't be silly – you're alive. And anyway I don't particularly want to see you in a glass case.'

'You want me to die, though. Isn't that what you want?'

'–'

'And at the same time you don't really want me to die. You want to hold on to both. If I were to tell you, here to your face, that I have no intention of killing myself, then I think you'd be at a loss. At the moment you think you can will me to die, but if I refused you couldn't let go: you would be forced to try and kill me yourself. And if you succeeded you would also lose. You would lose the thing that keeps you alive. Just like the fisherman.'

'You think very highly of yourself.'

'It's not about me, it's all about you. All about you and the others. The whole lot of us were more dead than alive, before we found a reason to live. I am that reason. My death is that purpose. Without it you do not exist.'

'You're crazy.'

'Fine, I'm crazy. Forget all about it. Anyway, it too late.'

'Why's it too late?'

'Because I've decided enough is enough. I've made the decision to kill myself.'

'Don't be so dramatic. You don't have the guts. And if I thought you did I would stop you. It would take more than a common cold to kill you.'

'But I am the trout. The trout is more astute than the man. I will always succeed where you will fail, simply because you are playing my game, and I am the one who is making the rules. This isn't a cold I've got...'

'What?!'

'That's right. You're going to lose. I'm ending the game, just like the trout, because I've decided I've had enough. You can do what you want. You can stay here forever and rue on what was. But now you will be on your own.'

'Rubbish. You can't die. You're not going to die. What is it if it isn't a cold?'

'Do you want to know? Do you really want me to tell you?'

'Yes, damn you!'

'Well then. I swallowed the rest of the sleeping pills which poisoned Prue.'

'No, you didn't.'

'Yes, I did.'

'You didn't!'

'Look, this isn't a pantomime. If you don't believe me then sit here and watch. It shouldn't take very long.'

'How long ago did you take them? I don't believe you. I can't believe you. You haven't got the balls. This isn't a game, it's a lie. You said that Prue died quickly.'

'That's true, she did. Ten minutes or so. But think of the difference between her and me. I'm younger, and maybe three times her size. It will take a lot longer with me. In fact it's taken longer already. Since you knocked on the door it's been... let's see... thirteen minutes.'

Charles came over to me. He looked into my eyes. His face was crimson, blotched and raw; stupid with uncertainty. He felt my pulse, and then my brow. He grabbed the bottle from my hand and shook it, listening out for sound. Then, in a madness, in a fury, he stuffed fat fingers down my throat and tried to make me sick. He spat at me; he slapped my face. Then, in despair, he let me go; he watched my body fall and sink into the pool of eiderdown. He sat down on the bed beside me. Right on the edge. His head in his hands.

'How long has it been?'

'Nineteen minutes.'

'When will you go?'

'I don't know. Never done this before. Ten minutes maybe. Can't feel my legs.'

'What am I going to do?'

'_'

'What am I going to do now?'

'Do what you want. It's your life. Up to you.'

'You bastard.'

'Good luck. You're on your own from this point. Nice knowing you, and all that crap.'

'What am I supposed to do?'

'Go fishing…'

'Supposing… just supposing you're right, how can I go on living like this? I don't mean money or somewhere to live. I mean having a reason to want to live. Something that makes me get up in the morning; something to fill my mind. Do you know what I mean?'

'_'

'All right. Maybe what you're saying is true. Maybe you think that you've won. This is your idea of a laugh.

Because you're going to leave me here, abandoning me on my own. Is that it? Well, you're wrong. You think you're clever, but you've got it all wrong. I've got ten minutes to prove you wrong. And by hell and damnation I'll do it. That's just enough time to kill you myself, and then put an end to it all.'

'Could you do that? Kill both of us?'

'I don't know. I… I think I could kill you.'

'Then kill yourself?'

'Possibly. Maybe. How hard can it be?'

'Swallowing pills was easy.'

'Was it? Is it? Are you really going to die?'

'Yes, I am. That's the truth of it.'

'I think, perhaps, I could swallow some pills.'

'No go. Sorry. Finished the bottle.'

'Damn it. You did. How many did you take?'

'I didn't count. Plenty. Enough for the job.'

'And how are you feeling?'

'Like shit.'

'_'

'_'

'Sod it, Martin. I can't kill myself. I've always been frightened of death.'

'Fine. Have a warm bath instead.'

'Don't take the piss! Just don't take the piss! You're lucky – you're dying. But I've got nothing. There's nothing left. No consolation.'

'Not taking the piss. Do it in the bath.'

'Do what in the bath?'

'Slit wrists. It's painless. Like falling asleep.'

'It might be, but I still couldn't do it.'

'Don't have to. I could.'

'You could?'

'Yes. Do you a favour. Go out together. Not much time. You choose.'

'Shall we? No, it's crazy. Give me time. Why the fuck didn't you tell me this yesterday?! Why didn't you give me time to think? This is all part of your game, I suppose. Maybe I won't have a reason to live. Maybe I will go out of my head when you're dead. There again, I may not.'

'Need to decide, old man.'

'Give me a chance to think! Give me a little bit longer!'

'As long as you like. I'm out. Make decision yourself.'

'No! Don't go! Don't go, Martin!'

'Not conscious much longer. I'm sorry.'

'_'

'_'

'All right then. Let's do it! Let's do this thing!'

'_'

'Martin! Help me! Let's do it!'

'Bath.'

Charles ran into the bathroom next door. I could hear the wheezing of opening taps. I could hear the sound of the plug on its chain, striking a tune against the enamel, being placed clumsily into the drain. I could hear the sound of bubbling water filling the coffin where he was to lie. Then Charles was once again by my side.

'I'll crawl over. Get ready. Find blades.'

'Where are they, Martin? Where are they?'

'Cupboard behind mirror.'

Charles hurried into the bathroom. I could hear him opening the cupboard door. I could hear his clothes as they dropped to the floor. The sound as he stood in the steaming bath, as he sunk his body into its own.

I got out of bed and walked to the door. Then I lowered myself to my hands and knees and crawled round the curve of the skirting board, over the tiles, towards him.

Charles was already submerged to his neck. He looked excited but pale. He was trying to process what was happening, but events were occurring too fast. All he knew was that he needed to act before he was left on his own. I could see it in the look of relief which passed across his anxious face as he saw me crawl round the door. He turned off the taps and smiled at me. Such a childlike smile. So innocent.

'Thank god you made it. You ok?'
'Of course not. Numb.'
'The blades are here. Don't miss, Martin. Christ, don't miss. Christ! Bloody hell! Half an hour ago I was looking forward to supper.'

Charles started as I came towards him, still on my knees and palms. I think he felt an urge to get out; an urge to escape. He was splashing about. I really don't know what he felt.

I crawled up to the side of the bath, unsheathed the blade, and dug it into his wrist.

'Bastard! Bastard, Martin!'

I pushed his hand beneath the water; I pointed to his other arm. He held it away, clutched close to his chest, unwilling to yield it up. He looked back down at his wounded limb, watching the water cloud with blood – a quizzical look upon his face, as if he was trying to comprehend.

I crawled to the loo and hauled myself up until I was hunched on its seat. I groaned. He turned his eyes in my direction, glad to see I was dying too. Those eyes of his, so full of fear, filled with the promise that they would see the end of me and watch me die.

'How long?'

'Thirty two.'

'Ha! Not long to go, you old shit. This isn't your victory. It isn't yours any more. This is ours.'

'_'

'I wish I'd had more time. There's so much I think I needed to do. There's so much I should have done.'

'_'

'Have you made a will? Did you say goodbye to anyone? Who will cry when I've gone?'

'_'

'_'

'_'

'Forty seven! You alive, Martin? You still there?'

'_'

'Who do you think will go first?'

'_'

'Shit. It might be me, Martin. You know, it might be me. I'm all weak. Is this a good way to go, Martin? Is it? Tell me! It's all mixed up. It's all wrong. I think I want out.'

'_'

'You dead, Martin? Who's first, do you think? Who first?'

'You, I expect.'

I stood up. I looked at him intently.

'Yes. Definitely you.'

'_'

'I didn't take them, Charles. No. I didn't take them.'

Charles clawed at the rim of the bath. But in truth, his strength was gone. He was hellish pale.

'Plug me up, Martin, you bastard! Plug me up!'

I took pity on him and attempted to do so, though knowing my efforts were too late. He expired with no noise, warm and relaxed, in the molten heart of my bath.

I rose and walked back into my bedroom. I opened the door to the hall. I wanted to call Harry up from downstairs, but I found he was waiting for me in the shadows. It was time for supper, he said.

I ate in the dining room, all on my own. Harry brought me a large portion of lamb, served in an excellent sauce. Then, with two glasses of red wine inside me, I retired to my study and lit a cigar. I started to make some notes of this story, and this is where I am writing it now.

Charles has been bumped down two flights of stairs, and only Harry knows where he's gone. Only Harry knows where his body – along with the bodies of all of the others – has come to a final rest. Harry knows all that is to be known, though he keeps his confidence close.

~

And now I search for a fitting conclusion. I thought perhaps, once the deed was done, I would feel remorse, or loneliness. I would find myself as I threatened Charles – as sore as the fisherman in my tale.

But it is not so. Charles was not a worthy opponent. He annoyed me with his hints and suggestions, so blunt once

I knew he lacked the strength to stand against me like the others. To stay true to his purpose; to see it through. In truth, I am glad he is gone.

You may think that now I am here on my own I will atrophy and lose all desire for life and for living: I will fade away. But that is not as I plan it. I have cast myself as the fisherman, but not the man I described. Instead, I shall simply move to new rivers, and go in search of more succulent fish. The greater challenge will inspire me to action, and the trout I caught was not so big that it can't be bettered by those to come.

This is my house; I am master of it. At this very moment Harry, my man – death's summoner, and the devil's apprentice – is drawing up offers to others I know. His invitations urge them to stay, indefinitely and free of charge. I am rich enough that they won't refuse. I will take small groups, and begin again.

While he writes I am watching the late summer twilight shrink within the mantle of night, and the final crimson threads of day dissolve beneath a ponderous sky. I am drawing on an exquisite cigar, dressed in a nightgown, sipping a brandy, enjoying the pleasure, the glorious feeling, of being truly alive.

When I Was Young

She never thought she was beautiful. She never thought of it at all.

'O, what a darling child!' 'What a lovely little girl!' Her cheek was pinched, her hand was pressed, her shoulders squeezed, her body lifted up in strong hands locked around her waist. This nuisance was a part of life; she never thought it more. She yielded when it took her mood, and when it didn't she would fight, or merely shy away. She didn't care for what they did, nor what it was they had to say. Not often did she care. And then, when she was old enough, she learned to run away.

'Stop it!' 'Get off!' 'Don't touch me!' She was one of the boys, and did as boys must do. To her mother's despair she fought at school, in the playground and in class. She fought at home. She learned to slam, and swear, and slate. To break things, take things, hide things somewhere no one thought to look. She even learned to spit. 'Everyone spits and swears at school!' 'It's not fair to lock me in my room!' 'O! How I hate you all!'

She was caught cheating in exams. 'You mustn't ever do that again! You're a lovely little girl, and so pretty. Pretty little girls shouldn't do such things.' Then only ugly people could cheat. She envied Angela for that. Angela was so ugly. Everyone knew it, they told her so. They ganged up on her, despised her, mocked her because she was so ugly. But how enviable she was too! Being able to cheat in exams! She envied Angela's broken glasses; she envied her crooked nose; she envied her chin which went on forever; she envied her red buckled shoes.

One night she stole the kitchen scissors. She went to the bathroom, and there in the darkness she chopped off all of her hair. All she could grasp on the back of her head – all that cascaded over her cheeks – till her ears and her neck were bare. Now I have hair like Angela's hair, so I will be able to cheat in class. But she found out it wasn't so. Then what was the point of being unattractive? Why did people decide to be ugly if there wasn't something in it for them?

And anyway, it didn't work. Despite the punishment, the bribes, the coercion – the incessant 'don't ever do that again!' – her mother's friends still said of her, 'O, what a beautiful girl!'

She ran to her room and looked in the mirror. Why aren't I ugly now? Why don't they mock me for having short hair? She pushed her face up close to the glass, inspecting all she could see. Her hair was much like Angela's, and her chin was almost as long. When she felt with her finger along her nose she knew that it wasn't straight. Perhaps wearing glasses made people ugly. That's what she needed to do.

She crept downstairs in the small of the night, searching within the drawers in the hall, where sunglasses were hidden behind a scrunch of hats and gloves. She took the ugliest pair.

At school next day she hid in the toilet, and broke the lenses against the bowl. At last she'd have proof of her ugliness; at last she could enjoy their scorn.

She balanced the empty rims on her nose and went back into her class.

'Where did you get those?' her teacher demanded.

'I need to wear them,' she replied.

'Don't be stupid, girl! There aren't any lenses in them.'

'Yes, there are.'

'Go into the corner this minute! I can't abide foolish children!'

She sat in the corner, alone, triumphant. Surely they'll hate me, surely they'll mock, because now I am ugly like Angela. Though when the bell for break-time sounded, when she ran out onto the tarmac, when she put on the glasses once more, nobody came to hit her or spit at her, nobody laughed at or called her names.

'Simon! Simon!' she shouted, tugging at the sleeve of a body swinging from the bright yellow bars of the climbing frame. 'Simon, am I ugly?'

'I don't know.'

'Tell me! Am I ugly? I want to know!'

'All girls are ugly!' he replied. But she knew he was just saying that.

'Then why don't you say something nasty to me?'

'Leave me alone! I want to swing!'

So she left him alone and went to another. She asked the same question once more –

'James! Hit me, James! I'm ugly! Please hit me!'

'If I do, will you hit me back?'

'It depends how hard you hit me.'

'How hard do you want me to hit you?'

'I don't mind… But not too hard. If you hit me too hard I'll hit you back.'

'Then I won't. You hit people far too hard. I don't like it when you hit me.'

'I promise I won't.'

'No, I don't believe you,' cried James, and ran to the shelter of the teacher.

Later, at home, she sat in the lounge and stared at the fire, vexed by a knowledge she couldn't acquire. Why didn't James hit me when we were playing? He didn't hit me because he knew I would hit him back if he hurt me. I hit people back, but Angela doesn't. Angela's ugly because she's weak. Then I must be pretty because I am strong.

'Daddy, why am I strong?' she swiveled round and asked of a sudden.

'I beg your pardon?'

'Why am I strong?' she moaned impatiently.

'Because you fight too much. I thought your mother told you to stop fighting.'

'Yes, but if I stop fighting then I'll get all ugly like Angela.'

'What?!'

'If I don't fight my chin will get longer, and I'll have to wear glasses, and…'

'Rubbish! Who on earth told you that?!'

'Angela never hits anyone, and she's disgusting to look at.'

'That's a nasty thing to say, and it's not true! Being strong doesn't make you attractive. Gentle women are often thought beautiful. Look at your mother…'

'Yuk! She's old and all wrinkled!'

'She's beautiful. The older she grows the more gorgeous she gets…'

'O, Dad! When she's as old as Granny she'll be revolting!'

'Not to me she won't. You'll find the same for yourself. Your attitude will change. You'll see', he concluded enigmatically.

Not for the first time in her life she left the room unsatisfied, appalled at her father's lack of perception, stunned by his ignorance.

~

If there was one thing more irritating than being called 'a beautiful girl' it was being called 'a beautiful woman'. Yet she felt herself changing, developing. She looked in the mirror with intrigue and foreboding, wondering how all these changes were happening while she stayed the same in herself. Yes, Angela was bloody ugly. She'd need a beard to disguise that chin. Though even then she would still be ugly. What made Angela so plain? And why, by contrast, was she thought pretty – without even having to try.

The attitudes around her altered. She walked down the street and sensed herself watched. She could feel the scrutiny of men. And then, the contest to impress; the eyes, the smiles, the innuendos; the invitations, gifts, false laughter; the awkward silence, the skin-deep banter; pressing ever closer, closer; harmless, hurtful words and gestures; fingers, hands, and lips, and shoulders. She hated all of it.

At sixteen she recoiled at the thought of eighteen. At eighteen she didn't dare to think what life would be like at twenty-one. At twenty-one she felt twenty-five was more than a lifetime away. Yet all too soon she found herself thirty, and still she thought herself to be young.

Angela had surgery on her eyes. Her nose settled comfortably into her face and almost seemed to become her. Even her chin was less pronounced, as if its protrusion was chiseled away. It must have been. Certainly her boyfriend thought so, or he wouldn't have dared to propose. Or then to go on and marry her; to love her for who she was. Then, not long after, they had their first child. And then, she was pregnant again. All whilst Angela's old school friend marched on alone, and all on her own, carrying her beauty forever before her – a banner, a headline, a shield.

And then, almost before she knew it – as though it had crept up behind her in secret and breathed its brave truth on the back of her neck – she had reached the age of thirty-five.

Then, when next she looked, she was forty.

She was godmother to Angela's third child. She went to the christening, and found that the men were not all looking at her. Their eyes were elsewhere, not always upon her. Their gaze seemed to wander around the room. Well, here there were girls of twenty-one. Mere children; lanky and pale.

After the christening she went back home.

'Hello, my beautiful!' said her father, greeting her with his open arms.

She submitted herself to his rapture in silence, thinking his welcome a slight. He calls me his, the one he finds beautiful, not the one who is known to be beautiful – not as once, as it was before. When I was the only one in the world – more gorgeous, more beautiful than them all.

So she stopped in the mirror, she looked in the mirror, ever and often inspecting its gaze. She looked and she saw and she said to herself – I'm forty now, yet my skin is so soft, and my eyes are sparking and clear. Hardly a blemish, hardly a wrinkle spoils my beautiful face. Angela may be tired and worn, but I am beautiful, still I'm beautiful. I am the beautiful one.

The Very Peculiar History of Hamish Anderson

Ask anyone you know who has died, and they will tell you the biggest shock is finding out about it.

Hamish Anderson is a case in point. He was quietly reading his morning paper over a leisurely English breakfast when he came across his obituary. Despite the generous portrait painted – depicting a man he scarcely knew, if it wasn't for the photograph – he wasn't chuffed in the least.

He phoned up the local paper at once, wanting to lodge a complaint. Only to be told by some junior clerk that he was the third Hamish Anderson to have called and protested that morning. Far from signaling misreportage, they deemed the multiple grievances as indubitable evidence of his demise.

Hanging up on the junior clerk, Hamish decided it best to retrieve his reputation, his health, and his life with the help of an intermediary. He would call his old friend Smith. Smith would understand his plight; Smith would champion his cause.

Smith. Yes, it was Smith, a familiar voice affirmed at the other end of the line. And who was he? Why, he was Hamish. You know. Hamish. Golf trips, fishing trips, midnight dips. Hamish. Your old chum. Come on, Smith. Wake up, Smith. Smith, wake up!

Smith's voice crackled over the line. Slowly, uncertainly, coming to life. Hamish. Yes, it could almost be Hamish. That voice – his voice – had a certain resemblance. He could almost believe the person was Hamish. When he closed his eyes, he imagined it was. But then, of course, that was quite absurd. It couldn't be Hamish. It wasn't Hamish. It simply couldn't be him.

'And why not', a petulant Hamish replied.
'Because he was buried yesterday. I went to his funeral.'

Before there was time to question Smith further, before he could prove beyond all doubt that he, Hamish Anderson, really was Hamish – foolish, preposterous though that was – the line in his hand went dead.

Hamish dithered in the hall, pondering who to call next. He let the handset fall to the floor; he sat down, frustrated, beside it. For the first time, perhaps, in the whole of his life, Hamish doubted himself. Could it be possible he wasn't Hamish? Could it be possible he wasn't alive? Picking up the phone once more, he dialed an enquiry line.

'Dalbeattie.' 'Anderson.' 'Hamish Anderson.' 'Thank you.' 'Good bye.'

And in that call there were vital clues. The person on the other end had heard him speak and answered him. That meant that he was alive. And there was more good news. The number that was given him for Hamish Anderson – the man he asked of from Dalbeattie – matched the number of his phone. The phone he was holding in his hand. Which would suggest, beyond all doubt, that he was Hamish Anderson. The phone was Hamish Anderson's. The house was Hamish Anderson's. He, Hamish, was an Anderson. He could be no one else.

The sheer relief to know he was the man he was, and still alive – despite whatever Smith might say – consumed him with such happiness: with urgent, unspent pride. It urged him walk around the town and flaunt his new-found Hamishness. To shout it out so all could see that Hamish was alive.

Though, now that he had been transposed from this world to the one which waits – forcibly removed and placed, if only briefly, with the dead – Hamish thought it might be fun to eke out the pretence. To hold out dead. To phone his friends and spread the news. 'Anderson has popped his clogs. The old boy's gone at last.' He would commiserate, he would postulate, he would speculate over the will. He was eager to do it, if only to learn what those who were close to him thought he was like. Then, after playing dead for a while, when the game had tired and lost its sheen, he would amble casually into the club; he would have a drink, a game of bridge. He would float it into the conversation. 'How are you doing, old man?' 'Not bad. I died last week, but it wasn't too painful.' 'Did you? That's tough. Can I get you a gin?' And it would go on that way for hours, till somebody realised he shouldn't be there. And when they did, that would give an excuse to party all over again. 'Hamish! How lovely to see you! Splendid funeral! You are looking better for it…!'

Hamish paused amidst his thoughts. So there must have been a funeral. Smith couldn't have gone to a burial unless one had actually taken place. If so, then someone must have died. There must have been a corpse. Then who had Smith seen stuffed in a box? Who had he lowered into the grave? Whose was the coffin? Whose was the body? Might it not have been Hamish?

The thought of it was pure madness. He needed to get a grip of himself. To pinch himself to make sure. Spectacles, testicles, wallet and watch. Yes, he was here, and in his own body. He was alive, of course. Though that didn't stop some other Hamish – someone unknown who shared his name – from being removed from this world.

And what was so strange about that? There are hundreds of Scotsmen who share the same name. Hundreds of Scotsman who die each day.

Hamish glanced at the paper. He had been mistaken for somebody else, in a different place with another complaint, who happened to have the same name. That was all. One was alive, and the other was dead. He should have gone to the church himself. That would have quashed the confusion at once.

Then why, thought Hamish, didn't I go? After all, if people like Smith had found out, I should have done so too. Where have I been for the last few days?

Hamish conceded that for the last week he had kept very much to himself. He hadn't been out for a game of golf; he hadn't gone down to the club. It was possible, now that he gave it some thought, that he hadn't been seen by a soul. Then surely all he needed to do, to dispel this mystery once and for all, was to open the door and stand on the porch. Before very long Mrs Poole would be sure to poke her head out and see him. To see him and scream, and within half an hour most of the village would know.

That was all he needed to do.

It was so simple, so certain, so utterly Hamish.

On the way to the door he caught sight of himself in the glass. Yes, I'm Hamish. Of course I'm Hamish. Hamish Anderson lives.

The mid-morning sun was peeping through the lattice of laurel which grew in the garden, as Hamish leisurely paced the porch, waiting for Mrs Poole to appear, to peer round the corner and see him.

~

Hamish Anderson, as he insists on calling himself, has been charged with breaking and entering the house of Hamish Anderson, deceased.

When the Time is Right

I was sitting with Sam Sullivan in Gatwick airport. There's a nice little bar tucked away in the corner of the mezzanine overlooking the concourse; it has comfortable armchairs, and an air of privacy more befitting a club. We had been there for over two hours.

If I had to choose a companion to idle away a couple of hours, then undoubtedly I would choose Sam. Not just because he's my oldest friend, but because he's such good company. His smile is infectious. He draws people round him; he is most at ease when right in the heart of a crowd. In his job as a foreign correspondent he has travelled well and come across people from every walk of life. His stories are legion. They can stretch the imagination sometimes, though they are too enticing not to believe. You warm to him, you instinctively like him, you trust him, you want him to be your friend.

Just as I wanted his friendship then. To amuse me with his fabulous tales; to distract me from the coming flight. Knowing with him I would be all right.

I have never been good at traveling by air. I don't like not being in control. In being so far removed from the ground that were an accident to occur then there is no chance of survival. Turbulence terrifies me. The mere shake of the wings. The worst bit is the anticipation – the thinking of flying before it occurs. And the closer I come to the day of the flight, the nearer I get to the terminal, the more apprehensive I am. I have a ritual I perform as soon as I get to an airport. I go to a bar for a large Bloody Mary. I pretend it will make things all right.

Only this time it didn't. The flight had been delayed by two hours. I had drunk a number of Bloody Marys, and they hadn't calmed my nerves in the least. In fact, they were making things worse.

Sam was doing his best to amuse me. He was pacing me drink for drink, in a show of solidarity. He had been through a repertoire of tales; he had done all he could to diminish my fear through logic, deflection and common sense. I could see he was starting to tire from the effort of humouring me.

For once he seemed vulnerable. Open to closer scrutiny. Open to opening out himself. For Sam was one of those sociable people who never let you into their lives. Who live that curious paradox, of staying well-hidden while in full view. Only a handful of very close friends – of which I prided myself to be one – had seen through Sam's charm and recognised that despite all the stories, the people, the laughter, he never spoke of himself. Though I knew him well, there was much of him that I knew I did not know. So much he seemed reluctant to tell. Even to his long-suffering wife, I think he remained an enigma.

So, fuelled by a cocktail of fear and drink, wanting some form of pleasing distraction, I tried to tease him out –

'I don't like the idea of dying.'
'Of course not. I've never met a person who does. Death is inevitable. Face it. It has to happen.'
'I know that. But I want a good crack at living first.'
'All of us do. That's natural as well. The present is what it is all about. Where it's at. We all like being alive.'
'And when it does happen, I don't want it to be an accident.'

'Do you mean to happen in an accident, or by accident?'

'An accident is an accident…'

'No, it's not. Not necessarily.'

'What do you mean?'

'I don't mean anything. I mean, I'm reconciled to the idea of death, even though I don't like it, because I'm coming round to the notion that death can't be accidental. Even though an accident may be what causes it.'

'That doesn't make sense.'

'I think it does. I've… I've started to develop my own little theory. Something private that I keep to myself, which I'm beginning to accept as a truth. Something that makes death easier to think about and to face up to, even when it occurs. And the best thing about this theory, of course, is that I have no way of proving it wrong. Not, at least, until I am dead, by which time I won't care.'

'Tell me.'

'I'm not sure I want to. I've never told anyone this. It's a work in progress.'

'Then you can perfect it by sharing with me.'

'It's not at that stage of development yet.'

'That doesn't matter. It will evolve in the telling. I promise to keep it under my hat. Look, I really don't want to get on this plane. My mind's doing cartwheels right now. The longer we stay here the worse it will get. Drink doesn't steady my nerves: it increases the paranoia. If you have a theory that might reassure me, then share it with me in confidence. Please.'

'I can't reassure you of anything for certain. It's nothing more than a theory.'

'I don't care. I like theories. Please.'

'Well, much the same as you, I don't like the thought of dying by chance. And by that I don't mean death in an accident, but death that isn't supposed to occur.'

'Supposed to?'

'Yes. Because my time has not yet come.'

'Your time?'

'I like to think we live our lives until we are ready to die.'

'What do you mean by that? Are we talking about God?'

'No, this isn't about God, though it can be if you want it to be. It's about whatever is right for the individual.'

'If people are brought into the world by chance, shouldn't they go out the same way?'

'Is it chance that put you on this earth?'

'My birth was a chance of nature, surely.'

'In natural terms, yes. The chemistry was entirely chance. Yet now you are here, and this is your time. And I don't think that is coincidence.'

'I knew you were going all fatalistic on me.'

'I'm not. And it's not religious either. If anything, it's heretical. It's a selfish theory, to persuade myself that I won't go by mistake. I don't believe in life after death. I think that when my body dies my mind must die too. But I also like to think that all of us die at a certain time. Perhaps once we've gained an understanding, or done something good. Or maybe nothing at all. Whatever it is, we can't be cheated; we cannot die by accident – not before it is ready and proper. Before we have reached the point that we must. However wise and grey and old; whatever we might have accomplished.'

'You think we must have accomplished something; there must be a purpose to why we are here?'

'No, we don't need to do something great. Most people don't, and that's fine. But we need to complete our lives. To die when we're ready.'

'You need to be more specific.'

'Of course. Can you remember when I used to cycle to work – about three years ago?'

'Before your accident, yes.'

'Yes, that accident. Can you remember?'

'You were hit by a car. You were fine.'

'I was fine, yes – as it turned out. But I was cycling too fast when I came down the hill; I hit black ice and my brakes were useless; I sailed through the lights, and was hit by a car going at forty miles an hour.'

'You were fine.'

'Fine. If that's what you choose to call it. I remember the curious sensation. Of being detached from the bike; of being hurled forcibly up in the air; of landing on my back in the road. Almost as though I'm a casual observer – a witness of my own destiny. Watching it in a slow motion movie. The arc of my body; its unnatural flight; the sound and the weight as it hits the road. And then real time returned. I remember sitting and looking about me; I remember seeing my bike all twisted; I remember feeling over my body, wondering why there was no breakage, wondering how there could be no blood.'

'You were lucky, that's all.'

'There is luck, and there's something that goes beyond luck. Something not about luck at all. Something inevitable. I had a feeling all the way home, which continued for many days after the smash. A feeling, a knowing, a realisation that I should have been severely injured. No. That I should have died, right there on the road. Instead, I was still alive.'

'You said you led a charmed existence.'

'That was my first reaction. Yet, since starting to build this theory of mine, there is something else I recall. Something I didn't consider back then, because it seemed a trivial detail. Though now I see how important it is. How it is the key to everything else.'

'What is?'

'I remember being hurled in the air, I remember being surrounded by people, but what I have no memory of is that moment between the actual crash and becoming aware of the accident. There was a strange little hiccup in time, in which I apparently thought or did nothing. In which I didn't exist. There was a blank, an indefinite pause. The bike was being crushed beneath me, buckling under the weight of the car, and I knew my life was as good as gone. Then, when next I was aware of myself, it was over. I was lying on my back on the tarmac; I was lying unhurt, and alive. I knew I had cheated death in some way.'

'It happened so quickly you can't remember it all.'

'No. I had a reprieve. Had I died it would have been a mistake; death would have occurred before my time. Yet, simultaneously, I knew that I should have died right there. Those two truths are irreconcilable. Sure, you can pass it off by saying I'm lucky; you can put the whole thing down to chance. You can say that momentary blackouts occur – they are part of life, of who we are. But I don't believe that's what happened to me. Not then, and not before. Because there have been other occasions, too. I remember I ran in the father's race for my eldest son at school. I got to the finish and was so knackered that I collapsed on the ground and struggled for breath. There was a moment when I couldn't breathe. I felt it then, too – the knowing. I felt my life was slipping away; my body preparing itself to go. I remember thinking, over and over, 'Christ, this is a dingy way to die'. Then the same hiccup; the same fracture in time. And then, the next instant, I was being propelled back into the world, hauled off the ground by his Latin master, as though I was starting all over again. Surely you've felt that feeling yourself? That proverbial moment when the car appears and hurtles towards you as if from nowhere; that realisation the car can't stop before it comes into contact with you. That certain sensation when closing your eyes, of knowing that you can do nothing to stop it – that nothing can pluck you out of its way. And then, the next instant, whether you have been hit and have somehow survived, or the car has swerved and not hit you at all, you somehow escape from the clutches of death. Somehow. That is the word. Some outrageous, fortuitous luck when the moment of crisis arrives. When we stare straight into the face of death. An accidental death maybe, but one we can see no way to escape from, no natural means to avoid. That is not a charmed life. That is an unworldly one. It has happened to me about four or five times; and that is too often for chance. Then what if not chance? And why? And how? The conflict remains – I should have died, yet I didn't. Unworldly. That's what I thought for a very long time. In the dead of night I would sit up in bed; I would shiver, thinking 'I'm not so special'. What could it be if it was not luck; if I didn't believe in predestiny? Was I independent of man? Was the world my mind, and the things within it no more than a construct of mine? Was nothing real except me? And that's when my theory began to emerge. Being open to all possible worlds, so I could be true to myself.'

'What on earth are you talking about?'

'Good question. So this is the theory. Imagine that I live in World A. One day I fall in front of a train, and somehow I don't die. I don't, even though the circumstance demands that I would or I should have died. Somehow, I survive. I keep on living as I did before, whether injured or not it doesn't matter. What does matter is that I cheated death. Such ridiculous fate just doesn't make sense – it cannot make sense – unless we assume that I also die.'

'How can you possibly do both?'

'Therein lies the rub. I die in World A. Yet my death has been by accident; the time wasn't right for me. I must keep on living till I reach that point, that stage beyond where I am. And since I have died by mistake in World A, I simply continue to live in World B.'

'In Heaven?'

'No. On earth. In an exact replica of World A. The same people, the same places, the same things, the same jobs. Even the same demented old dog. Everything exactly the same; with an identical history right up to the moment when I die by mistake in World A.'

'So you die, and then you're reborn somewhere else?'

'No, I'm not reborn at all. I'm already there. I don't even realise I've died. The whole shift takes a fraction of time. There's a hiccup, a blank, an indefinite pause – so swift that I can't remember. I do not experience a transition: I'm there. Unconsciously my life continues within this latest identical world. And in that way I am preserved: I am spared till my time is right.'

'Whoa. So hold on. Even if there were identical worlds, your theory doesn't stack up. Say, for example, you die. What happens then? I commiserate for a while. There's a funeral, wreaths, the works. Then I get back to the business of living. Then a month or so later I'm hit by a brick; it cracks my skull open; I die. I move from World A to World B as you say – without being conscious that I have died – but then I find you're there as well, and still very much alive. It's nonsense.'

'You don't get where I'm going with this. There are no past worlds. When I die an accidental death the world where it happens must cease to be. It cannot continue to exist when faced with the paradox that I shouldn't have died, that something has happened outside what is right. That world is destroyed, and you with it – you in that world, that is.'

'That's a bit selfish of you.'

'Not really. I would experience the same fate if it were to happen to you.'

'So if I died by accident and it wasn't my time, the whole world would vanish and we'd all move on, seamlessly, to the next?'

'No. As I said, we don't move on. We're already there.'

'And what about that guy in the corner? What would happen if he were to die?'

'If he died by mistake it would be the same. We would all continue to live in the next.'

'And that's true for everyone?'

'Yes.'

'Then there must be millions of other worlds waiting for you or me or the man in the street to die into. There must be millions of you and me all living simultaneously!'

'That's true. It's simply a matter of scale. How many worlds do you want there to be? How many worlds do you think there are? There's no limit to the space or dimensions we live in.'

'There's a limit to how many of me there can be.'

'Why?'

'Well then, how many versions of me are there, Einstein?'

'An infinite number, and one.'

'So what are those countless versions of me doing as they sit in some future world waiting for someone to die by mistake?! God only knows!'

'God doesn't know. God has absolutely nothing to do with my theory. And anyway, you're not waiting. There may be billions of worlds out there, yet there can only be one of you. You are doing, of necessity, exactly what you are doing here, now, in this world we are living, within the greater universe of all worlds.'

'And is my World B the same as yours?'

'It has to be. We are living in a shared system of infinite worlds.'

'Then which me is the real me? Which world is the real world?'

'Ask yourself. Does this world feel real to you? Do you feel real within it?'

'Of course.'

'Then which one is real?'

'This one.'

'And the others?'

'You want me to say they are equally real.'

'I don't want you to say anything you don't want to.'

'But they are, aren't they? They are all real.'

'Yes, they are all exactly the same.'

'And limitless.'

'Yes.'

'Though imperfect ones have all been destroyed. When someone dies who shouldn't have died.'

'In essence, yes.'

'And there must be millions of those. I mean, people have accidents on a constant basis. We must be moving through the alphabet at a furious rate.'

'Yes, the speed is immense. But we are travelling through them without interruption, so we don't even notice the speed. Just as we don't notice how fast we are going as the world is spinning on its axis, right now.'

'It sounds chaotic.'

'Not at all. It makes sense of what otherwise struggles for meaning. Of what is arbitrary and beyond our control. Without wanting to mix metaphors, our shared existence is like a firework. Countless million particles of gunpowder are being ignited in close succession, driving us forward in one direction...'

'And then we are going to explode?!'

'No. Not an explosion. More of a realisation. Of something magnificent.'

'We can't all keep on living. And we don't. What happens when somebody dies? When they really die; when we see them die. When they don't continue in the next.'

'You know the answer to this.'

'They die because their time is right?'

'Yes.'

'Then that is the crux of your theory. We don't know when our time is right, but we know that until it is we are safe. We are spared an accidental death.'

'Yes.'

'It's a hopeful theory then.'

'Yes. It promises more than avoiding mistakes. It points towards a purpose. Think of that firework. It is heading in a consistent direction; it has yet to realise its potential; it will light up when that time arrives. And in the meanwhile all of mankind, collectively, are contributing to that common goal. We have to believe we are here for something. Even if we don't know what that is; however trivial it may be. We are bound in furious evolution, charging towards a natural perfection. There is something magnificent that awaits us, which we reach towards in ignorance. Something akin to a truth. We cannot be the sole aberration. Not in a world as perfect as this.'

'So we continue on till the time is right, individually and collectively. And do you think when the moment comes – just at the point when it's really right – we see, or discover, or become something else?'

'That is a different theory.'

'You have considered it too?'

'–'

'Tell me, how do we know when the time is right? Who decides when that is? And when it does come, when we really die, what do we move on to then?'

'These are too many questions. They are calling our flight.'

'Do you think you will know when your time is right? Do you think you'll be able to feel it?'

'We should go.'

'Will you tell me when the time is right? When you feel it is right for you. Will you tell me if you discover something? Some harmony, some balance, some truth. Will you find a way to communicate, either before or after you die?'

'Come. We have to go.'

'Will you promise to tell me…?'

~

But the time never seemed to be right. There was never the opportunity to return to that conversation. There was always something that came in the way.

Though I talked to Sam Sullivan often enough over the next few weeks and months to know that he had not abandoned his theory – but instead had refined it and countered its shortfalls – he never let me close enough to question him further on it. He was still a constant in my life, and as charming and witty as ever before, yet he never mentioned the theory himself. I felt, perhaps, that if he had wanted, he could have disengaged from distraction, he could have confided in me. Instead, he retreated into himself, back into the company of the crowd, from which I had teased him just once. I assume he had made a conscious decision not to entrust more to me. Perhaps because he had found something in it – something he didn't dare to reveal, or something that ripped the theory apart. I was eager to know the reason why, though I had promised myself not to ask. I was eager because I have to confess I had taken the theory to heart myself, I had worked upon it gradually in the intricate web of my mind. Slowly and steadily thinking it through, until it suited me well. It was something much more than an idle interest. A pattern to shape who I am.

Like him, I shared it with nobody else. Sam had laid out his soul to me in those last desperate moments of conversation, and I didn't want to betray his trust, to sully his theory in strangers' minds. I was wary, too, of revealing to him the extent to which I adopted his theory, adapting it to fit my demands. For that seemed a breach of confidence. Only once or twice was the topic raised. And on each occasion, before much was said, he gave me a look which warned me off, which seemed to accuse me of spoiling his faith, of tainting the system in which he believed. For that is what it had become. I am sure. He was consumed by conviction, engulfed in its glory, as only a man can be of a thing that he never dares bring to the light.

And, ultimately, I needed no more. For despite the frustration which brewed within me, I knew – beyond any doubt I was certain – he would tell me when the time was right. When the time was right for him.

Then he was given a foreign assignment, and I didn't see him at all. Beirut, Damascus, Amman. A series of challenging posts. So much so that he left the kids behind with Mary in England. For almost five years after we spoke I didn't see or hear of the man. His was a life that was full of adventure, loaded with mystery and intrigue. I wonder how many worlds he consumed as he found himself in accidents, when he would have died had his time been right.

Then, out of the blue, I received a call. Sam was coming back for a month, and Mary asked me to drive her to Gatwick so we could meet him when he arrived. Delighted, I said. So we drove to the airport, and I stayed in the car park while Mary took the kids to get Sam.

Shortly after, they came out of the building. I remember watching with envy. A family unit brought together after so many months. Sam was grinning and looking well-tanned. He had his arm around Mary. The two kids were clinging onto his coat. Nothing about him had changed. Nothing. He was the man I knew so well; the man I loved; the man who told me so little.

I got out of the car and waved. He saw me, and returned the gesture. He dropped his bag and stepped clear of the others, straight out into the road.

It was then the taxi hit him.

I saw it coming. I closed my eyes and searched for a blankness, a hiccup, a fracture in time. Yet none came. It was, as he said, like a slow motion movie. For when I opened my eyes again I could see the contact and hear the crack – that incredible crack as metal met man. Instead of flying into the air, Sam simply crumbled and fell to the ground, with the taxi wedged against his waist, and the foolish face of the blameless cabbie looking in shock at the crumpled heap of ruined clothes and bones.

I ran to Sam. A crowd had already started to form, and Mary was screaming, unable to stop. But we needed to speak – just once more.

'Is it time, Sam? Is this it?'
'I'm fine, old son.'
'Good. Good. But is the time right – has it come?'
'Don't worry. I'm fine.'

Sam winked at me.

I think he smiled. I think there was more he wanted to say. I know there was more to be said. But a crowd was surging all around him, and I needed to go to Mary.

By the time I had managed to soften her screams in the cold discomfort of my arms, Sam Sullivan was a corpse.

~

There was a small family funeral, and on its back a full memorial service. I have never seen so many people attending such an event. They flew in from across the globe. I learnt so much about my friend in a single afternoon. Whole chunks of his life which he had not shared, though I thought I had known him so well. I stood with Mary on the path which led away from the church. So many people shook her hand; so many people she had never seen or even heard of before.

That was Sam, through and through. He engaged with so many on such different levels that you didn't realise until he was gone how little he shared of himself.

I'm fine, he had said. What did that mean? What could that possibly mean? I could only interpret it one of two ways. He said he was fine because that's what he thought. He thought there would be a fracture in time, as he continued into World B. He would be waking up in a hospital bed, and I would be walking in with a beer concealed in the seam of my coat. I would be sitting down on his bed, and he would be talking about his escape – of how it proved his theory was true.

But he wasn't in a hospital bed. He had been cremated. So he didn't continue to live in World B. He was dead. Dead to the world. Dead in this world. Dead in every possible world. That being the case, the explanation had to be he had died. He had died because his time was right. He had come to a place, to a point in his life, where it all made sense; where he had no distance yet to travel; where he may have learnt or seen or felt some harmony, some higher truth. That was why he said he was fine – because he knew it was time.

Then I should feel happy for him. I should celebrate now he has gone. Why is it that I cannot do so? Is it simply that for those who are left we do not know what the other has found; we only feel the pain and the loss; we think of ourselves not of them? No, however selfish I am, it cannot merely be that. Sam's time could not have been right. He had been away from his family; after years he had just returned. He had hardly exchanged a word with his boys; he had yet to hold his wife in his arms: to feel the warmth of her touch on his skin, to feel her love pervading his soul. How could his time have been right?

What had occurred had not meant to occur. It so obviously happened by chance. It was a series of simple events, I learnt later, so randomly lethal, so banal in themselves, that it made a mockery of being his time.

Then there is a third explanation. Whatever Sam thought was going to happen, whatever he meant when he said he was fine, he was wrong because the theory is wrong. It is flawed. There is no system of infinite worlds. We live in chaos and are swayed by chance. We cannot cheat what we do not know. We go blindly into the darkness before us. We stumble, we hurt ourselves, and we fall. That is the only truth.

Then where does the theory leave me? I should reject it, disown it, for it is a lie. I should go back to being the person I was – the slave to fortune and fate. Living my life more carefully; knowing that when it is done it is done. Even in that final moment – that very point of non-entity – when neither dead nor alive. There is nothing to come. There is nothing to follow. There is no more. This is it.

And, above all, I won't delude myself by telling myself I'm fine.

That is what I must do, however much it hurts me to do it. That is what I am trying to do. If I can. Because it is wrong for being wrong. Because it doesn't seem fair. To be forced to regress. To deny myself the potential of being. To refute a purpose beyond the mundane. To return to the state of casual awakening in which Sam once found me and told me his lies.

Though his theory may have evolved. It may have moved on beyond the crude concept he shared when we sat in the bar. I am sure it had; he had shown me it had by avoiding the topic when we were together, by refusing to let me know more. I wonder how it may have progressed. I am certain he did not come to reject it; he was bound to have said if he had. Instead, I believe the reverse. It became a tenet by which he lived life; it wove within his fabric of being, entwining itself so intricately into everything he believed that you could not see it was there. It was indistinguishable from the man. Because of that he dared not speak it. He knew I must find it myself.

Then he was the greater fool for its failure.

Assuming, that is, it had failed.

Perhaps, after all, he was fine. The theory could have evolved in a way which allowed him to die and yet to continue – just not in the world that I know. He could still be alive, though hidden from me. He could be here, or somewhere different – somewhere within the universe of infinite possibility. But not dead. Surely, he could not be dead. Because his time was not right.

How could the theory do that? How could it let him keep on living when those who were left were left to grieve? Mary and their boys remained, lost in ugly ignorance, attempting to build back from the void that he created when he died.

I was still here.

Could he not reach out? Could he not say a word? Could he not reassure us in some way? He had promised me that he would.

His theory isn't a hopeful theory. It's an utterly selfish one. It torments us with uncertainty. It forces us to live our lives oblivious of what might be beyond what we can see. Uncertain even when we die of what awaits us next. There's no magnificence to that. No balance, no beauty, to be had. No firework shooting in the sky, about to burst with radiance, and show us to ourselves.

I look into the pitch of night; I strain my eyes; I seek to see. But all is emptiness. There is no truth beyond. No truth that waits. There is no more than this single moment, this fragile moment. There is only me, standing alone, standing within it.

Watching. Listening. Waiting.

The Muse Confused

Michael O'Connor was a genial man, who came amongst us of a night and never moved away.

He was raised in the city, so it seemed, but his manner was of country mould, and he heeded his nature well. He took the house by Flannigan's Farm, and charmed us with such pleasantry that we treated him as a prodigal. Nothing was known of his parentage, nor of his history. Indeed, what he did in the daylight hours, and how he earned a decent wage, was a total mystery. All we knew was what we could see – he laughed and joked and came to the pub; he chased all the girls for miles around, and forever wore a clear, broad smile.

That besides, it was plain to all that Michael was an industrious man, and very well learned he was, too. He chanted sayings as a bird pipes song, and his pockets burst their seams with books. Aristophanes, and Sophocles, and Aeschylus; Thucydides, Euripides, and more of these absurd long-sounding names.

At the age of twenty, or thereabouts, he married a girl called Maureen Flynn, whose head was well-placed on her shoulders, whose feet were firmly on the ground. She suited his nature not at all, for he was agreeably mad and wild, and she unerringly sane. But Flynns are a most mysterious breed, and dote upon antithesis. She took to Michael like a fire, and they loved one another well.

～

The first of their offspring was christened Katherine – her mother called her Katie – a red-haired bodkin, as fresh as the day, with keen bright eyes, and a voice like silk. The second was Lorna, and she was fair. Her hair was as gold as the weeping sun, and her pretty face shone like the blush of dawn. If ever a father was flush with joy, then Michael, it was he. Pride made him humble, and love made him strong. These traits he shared to shield the girls, and bond the family as one. The likes of him are sent to us to fill this fragile world with hope, to make us worthy of its care. God willed it so, and so it was.

Not many another full-faced moon had danced upon their happy roof before Mrs Chaney and I were woken one night by the drumming of fists on our door. I went downstairs to still the peace, and found the miscreant Michael. Maureen, he cried, as he pulled at our arms, was full in the throes with another child.

We came to the warm and panting house, leaving Michael by the hearth – snug in a chair with his daughters close – as we went about our chores.

It was four o'clock, and the fire was cold, when I sought him out again. It's another girl, I said. He smiled and unwrapped the girls from his lap; he tip-toed back the way I'd come till he was crouched at Maureen's side.

I have been all of a thought, said he, as she stroked his face with her hot, happy hands, and directed his gaze to the latest born. Let this one be called Atropos. Maureen frowned, too tired to talk or rally at his foolishness. She bent her weighted head to sleep, and nodded by his eager words.

Come morning, much to our dismay, he was still fixed upon his choice. For all that Maureen said against, for all she thought or sought to do, Atropos it was to be. This child, he cried prophetically, was given to us by the gods! My girls were sent to serve as Fates. They shall be as those ancient maids who spun men's lives upon their looms and measured out their destiny.

Maureen and I swapped eyes but kept our peace, knowing none had means to shake so forthright a decree. And neither could we afterwards. I went to church and heard it christened Atropos O'Connor. Poor purple-faced cub, so sorely named, screaming as the cross was made. And poor young girl who held her.

Yet that was not the final madness clouding Michael's mind. If they be Fates, he reasoned with his much and ever-loving wife, they must be tagged as such. So Katherine was repurposed Clotho; Lorna locked within Lachesis. Maureen took the girls aside and whispered soothing words. Clotho she distilled to Lottie, Atropos was swung to Amy; whilst that once Lorna stayed the same, for who could tickle forth a name from such a prison as Lachesis?

~

This stratagem enacted well when not in reach of Michael's ear. But when Atropos had learned to speak she spoiled the peace by telling him she far preferred her Fatal name to such a whine as Amy. Who calls you Amy? Michael asked, and all at once this close revolt was brought into the light.

A conference of young and old was called to settle the dispute. Michael ruled the day. Katherine was confirmed as Clotho; not as Katie or as Lottie! Atropos was Atropos: she wanted it that way. And Lorna... here he stopped and looked... and saw the child's head shook at him – that gilded, golden, gorgeous head – and those cheeks which were ever so white turned pale as she meekly stood her ground. Lorna, best beloved of all, apple of her father's eye. She must be Lorna and none else, thought he between his soul-sprung tears. And so it was to be.

Through the anxious, restless days betwixt O'Connor's nine-month year that ruled his house and set their world, he stalked his study, he became a troubled and a pensive man. His brow was furrowed; his eyes and ears would sometimes spurn and turn away from the song-filled upper rooms in which his children sat and cried. Maureen strove to please the man who doted on her yet so well, though even her soft hands were powerless to remove and smooth his scowl – until the time appointed came when he could claim the right to dub the next bright bairn Lachesis.

All things come to those that wait. And come they did; the next child too. I bathed and tended her myself. I saw the sun stroke back the worry wound around O'Connor's world, and crease the darkness into day. At last The Fates were three. Along with she who was called Lorna: apple of her father's eye.

But Fate is harsh. Whilst Michael danced to Destiny, his wife worked hard to weave a name to blunt the full force of Lachesis. Only Lottie sprang to mind, and that belonged to Katie. Days bred weeks that led to months, heavy with approaching storms. Lachesis grew a surly charge, and hankered ever for the right to name herself as Lottie. Maureen, fearful of a feud which would expose her subterfuge, convened a conference with her spouse, complaining none would wed such girls, whose names were held in such repute.

Michael pondered these wise words, then to his study he retired to browse amongst his dictionaries. After a while, the sage returned. He formed a circle of his girls, announcing that from this time hence they might be known as Furies. Maureen, thinking nothing worse than Lachesis, Atropos and Clotho, accepted in a trice.

Poor, wretched one! She little knew how great dismay could come of such assent. For in that instant they were scarred with brands so cruel they could not heal. The tyrant lovingly laid down his law upon them all.

On Katherine he imposed Allecto; Atropos, to her dismay – for dearly did she love her name – became a thing called Megaera; whilst Lachesis, with dignity astounding for her tender years, resigned herself to Tisiphone. Lorna, summer harvest, golden Lorna, apple of her father's eye, preserved her sole identity.

Would that Maureen had the chance to burn his books to dust! I saw despair wash round her eyes. Could any man but he she wed compose such doleful names?

A mother's fears are daughters' dreads – for aye they think the same and same times too. The moment Michael's back was turned, the girls sought refuge of Maureen, and begged for a reprieve.

A desperate woman is ingenious: God gives us means when Hope itself is trodden underfoot. Red-fire Katie she consoled by drawing Allie from Allecto. Megaera she sliced to Meg, thus stilling angry Atropos – who even learned, as months went by, the benefit of simple sounds. Whilst Lachesis, fresh to this sport, seemed quite content when Tisiphone translated into Tiffany.

With zeal the girls latched on to these, the clappers of those bells which tolled their cumbrous ties to ancient times. So well acquainted were they made with these new names that they would slip in careless moments – sometimes even within range of Michael's curious ear. He stood betrayal awkwardly, but loved them and his wife too well to force a fresh divide. His sole delight was bound to them – to be with them and watch them grow – but sounding them when time was slow with tidings of their Furious names.

~

Thus O'Connor might have passed his years a happy man, had Fate not sown in Maureen's womb the seedling of another child.

It was on another dismal night that Michael thumped upon our door, demanding that we came at speed to aid his wife once more. And mighty storm-tossed did I feel when down his stairs I trod at dawn to cast about the sticky news that yet another girl was born.

He winced at me with tortured eyes, for I knew as the village knew – we all knew, for he told us so – the Furies numbered three, not more. God willed it so, and so it was. And Michael must obey.

146

Maureen hid beneath the bedclothes, clasping close her precious chicks – Tiffany, Lorna, Meg and Allie – whilst Michael paced the floor below. He strode around in empty circles, seeking a solution which would crack the mystery. A man against a universe which stood opposed to all his plans.

At last an answer must have broke the dark which sheathed his clouded mind, and in that moment, with a cry, he leapt the stairs in pairs, and landed square in Maureen's room without so much as catching breath. With one bold stroke, one sweeping hand, he stripped the Furies of their names – those names they scarcely knew their own – and laid on them a greater charge, insisting each became a Muse.

The Muses number nine not three, chimed Michael to the patch of maids who clung about themselves confused, who could not reason if such news brought concord or more pain.

Another conference was called.

Katherine morphed to Calliope, the Muse of Epic Poetry, which Katie took and swiftly shaped – now being practised in the art – to the gentler-sounding Kylie. Atropos was more in tune, and asked her father for a list of all eight Muses which remained, so she might pluck from thence a name which played towards her like. She fixed upon Melpomene, the noble Muse of Tragedy, that with the gracious help of God she might remain plain Meg. And Lachesis, now Tiffany, chose Terpsichore, Muse of Dancing, with thoughts of much the same.

Michael once again sought Lorna: she, more beautiful than all, with hair the colour of the corn, with eyes which changed their shade to fit the manner of her mood. She, with giddy laugh and smile, who whispered love in every move, who flamed the hearts of all she met and burnt her warmth on every breast, as round she ran her dance of life. She, apple of her father's eye. But stubbornly she spun the sense that weighed upon her innocence. Lorna is the name you gave me. It is the name by which I'm known. Whims and moods may change my fancy, yet I'll answer Lorna still. Her father dared not stand against such truth, and such simplicity.

So remained the single child, the fragile bairn most recent born, which snuggled in the silk of sleep in Maureen's melted lap. For her he chose the name of Clio, Muse of ancient History. Maureen, wearied by the strain of birth, and tired of all the secrecy in which the girls' real names were veiled, took heart into her mouth and cried that she, at least, would claim the right to call her latest daughter Patty. This, she declared, could not offend, since it was short for Cleopatra: a figure out of history, a lovely creature of great beauty, as like as any to the very person of a Muse. Michael strung along with this, so pleased was he with such a wife – who could pop babes as shelling peas, whose mind could work ingenious ways.

God wove the web of peace anew, and Michael was a happy man. No longer did he pale at thoughts of Maureen bearing more. In fact, with health and youth intact, he saw no reason why they both might not complete the set. They needed but a handful more, and Lorna stood by in reserve.

Thus, scarcely days beyond nine months, I came again to Michael's house, along with Mrs Chaney. O'Connor's world seemed beautiful, and he was fat with joy. The thought of yet another Muse besieged his raptured mind. Yet when I tripped the waiting stairs to herald news of this next birth my heart was heavy in my chest, and so the hands which urged him wake.

It is a boy, I said with dread.

He strung with me into the chamber, greeting Maureen with a smile, and seeming not displeased. He said there was no need to fear. A son and heir would come in use. God knows it, to be sure. Maureen shook herself of blame; her disappointment fled. So greatly did she love her spouse, so greatly he loved her. Yet still she braced her anxious soul, prepared to hear the name he gave as nothing shy of Heracles. All round the dire expectant room the silence smote our women's hearts. Shall we not call him Michael? Michael posed.

Maureen struck the bargain in a trance.

Preparing for the podding of the seventh to this world, old Widow Chaney and myself made talk of Michael's ease – that he was pleased to have a son, and felt no slight that Maureen chose to undercut his daughters' names.

A foolish thing to gossip on, for seven also was a boy. When Michael heard he did not move: he sat as though a living statue, caught in silent disbelief. Then slowly he came back to life. He climbed the stairs and crept within the cosy chamber where they slept, but nothing did he say. And in that nothing we all knew that something was astray. Maureen had confounded him, denying him five Muses more. We saw it in his dreadful eyes although he tried to look away.

He worshipped her too keen to speak, except to name this latest Mickey. Yet that alone condemned her. Maureen's eyes were pools of dew which brimmed and surged across her cheeks the more she strove to hide. He folded her within his arms, he clasped her close upon his chest. Yet not before those soulless spheres had spat out oaths that all began 'if only I had died…'

Judge him the man who does but trip where Godless legions fall. Michael had but stumbled, and that past lay in his wake. He was restored before the morn, and bathed her sorrow with his words till she was bright again. He told her that their track was true, and beckoned those who boldly trod. They had four Muses in the bag, and Lorna might make five. These last few years were but a pause upon a path that would resume, fuelled by the hunger of their love. These honest words of truth restored composure in her ravaged soul. His consolation cheered her mood, and that was joy to him. Such things we are that never big should never be so small.

So passed the next nine vacant months, and Michael's life was full to burst, instructing Muses in their Art whilst sounding hope about his house. Calliope and Melpomene read Yeats and Shaw and Shakespeare every night; Terpsichore learned to dance; and Clio, though she could not read, had volumes of Thucydides beneath her counterpane. Even Maureen learnt anew: he tutored her to answer to Mnemosyne, despite the problems that it posed with spelling and pronunciation.

Fate greets us all in many guises; it comes in several shapes and sizes. When Mrs Chaney and myself were summoned next, a lucky stroke it proved to be that both of us were free. For in that afternoon there popped a gorgeous brace of girls. Michael cried, and fought back tears whilst bouncing on the bed, ordaining that these next be named Euterpe and Erato. Euterpe, Maureen whispered to the infant host that stood around, might find more comfort if called Julie. Erato could be none but Ratty. Both he and she were satisfied, and both were overjoyed.

Ten was a boy and was christened Michael, like the other two. A son, cried Michael, serves us well if but the past repeats its tune. Besides, nine charming burdens sat astride his busy days, and hung upon their idle fringe. He tutored all upon their art, and they displayed as best they could the learnings that he gave.

The next – a month short of a year – was Polyhymnia, Muse of Song. A vote was cast conclusively – eleven voices verses one – that she be known thenceforth as Polly. Although, of course, at Michael's hest she was baptized as Michael wont.

Michael was a man at peace. He looked about his happy hearth, and there he saw eight loving maids – the seven Muses and the other: she on whom fair nature doted – and stood beside them his three sons, united in a single name. And at their heart was Maureen Flynn: she the red-haired, she the beauty. She the woman whom he loved.

His one slight dread lay distant still. Both he and she were shy of forty by some several years. His calculations would suggest a danger of a tenth arrival of the female kind. And then, should there be ten to name, when knowing only of nine Muses, what would come of it? Should there not be a dozen maids – twelve seemed a more judicious sum. Or saving that, could he discern a larger group of girls? He conjured Sirens, Harpies, Sibyls, and counted up how they were numbered. Secretly, he sought their names.

Maureen was with child once more. Michael came and found me out, beseeching me to gauge its sex, or estimate if this be twins, that he might know the worst. I answered truly, with regret, that only nature could foretell, and she would keep her close lips sealed until the day of birth. We could do nothing more but wait, and put our faith in God.

This answer did not satisfy, yet Michael went his way, prepared to wait and then to learn upon the birthing day.

And so it should have been. Though, as the time grew near for Maureen to discover all, a different crisis caught them both.

One day, whilst in his silent study, O'Connor was surprised to find his bookcase tumble from the wall and plunge upon him with its weight of ancient tomes and wood. To other mortals such events would have had no great effect. Yet Michael's library was vast. His Muses and the three young lads took half an hour to dig him out. He did not suffer any break, but he was shaken to the core, and breath came awkward to his chest. He was, besides, a haemophiliac. I feared a haemorrhage from within, more vital than the cuts without which proved most hard to heal.

With but a whisker of two weeks till Maureen's proper time was due, her husband lay close by her side within that bed that I had served so frequently before. Around them Lorna and the Muses kept devotion night and day.

And it was on just such a night that Lorna crept up to his ear and begged to be a Muse. This, based upon a single birth, and that it proved a girl.

He nodded to her generous terms. In the dead of night the house was roused to witness this new rite. Lorna became Urania, Muse of the Astronomical – a title which she would renounce should Maureen pod twin girls.

Michael smiled away fatigue, content within his wretchedness, and slumped back on the bed. Fearing that he might be dead, the angels round him stood aghast and hid their crying eyes. Confused by such uncommon sense they had no feeling what to do, nor thought of what they did. Instead they kept their circle close around their best beloved.

That night, another child was born. Premature, and very small. Yet healthy; certain to survive. It was a girl. Its cries were the only noise in the room; its movements the only cast of life. Michael, reviving consciousness, held the baby in his arms. He named it Thalia, the Comic Muse. The last Muse of the nine.

Leant above him, tired and spent, Maureen planted one slow kiss upon his bloodless brow. Calliope, Melpomene, Terpsichore, Clio, Erato, Euterpe, Polyhymnia, the three boys, and Urania, stood in mute attendance. Then Michael's clasp on the infant locked. I was forced to tear the babe away.

Dawn was nestling on the drapes, and there was light beyond. The casual curtain flapped and waved; it sucked itself as a full-blown sail, as if to guide the waiting bark towards the underworld. The wind was neither callous nor cold; on its tail it bore a smiling sun. There were no shadows in this house. No darkness, and no pain.

Stood in silence by the bed, the three small boys paid homage to their father, and thus did the Muses to their god.

~

After the funeral came the christening. Kylie, Meg, Tiffany, Patty, Ratty, Julie, Polly and Lorna stood beside the three young lads, and marked the ritual well. The infant uttered not a cry, but smiled throughout. Its clear, wide eyes took in the world. All it saw was beautiful.

Maureen spared the babe her fate, and she was baptized Mary. Yet all her life they called her Thalia, and that was the only name she knew.

Carey

Behind the house a narrow track led out towards a hill. Used only in the autumn months when planters came to fell, it hid in tangled briars and bracken all the summer long. But all summer long, all through the year, a furtive path of naked feet was patted through its undergrowth. It danced through the scrub, it skipped round a pond, it bounded down an urgent slope, until it came to a tree.

Here the planters never came. Here, sheltered in a curvature, the tree stretched out, immeasurable, in one perpetual yawn. Its vast trunk bound around a boulder, covered with sheer spongy moss, woven in a short-cropped fleece, a shaven head of hair.

Standing on the primal stone you could stretch your arms and hug its frame, and the tree would shiver in pure delight – right to its fingers' ends. It would whisper to you as you wrapped around it, and from the knitwork of its limbs it sparkled sight and winked at you.

Beneath its shoulders, in the shade, the air was moist and cool. The ground beneath you swirled and shifted, plummeting to unknown depths, like a giddy, wind-whipped sea.

Only the stones were safe.

Outside, within the ticking heat, the bleached grass swayed like rhythmic seaweed, brought to life, in restless waves. The fine sky petered out of sight, distanced, lost upon the wind. The dots of random birds stood proud against its pastel tapestry – high in the ether, curling loose circles, scarcely flapping their wings.

And here, straight above me, through the infinite boughs that shot out like bridges, like elephants' trunks, like giants' fingers – clung to the air in the chattering canopy – swinging on sheaves of gossiping leaves, high in the treetop, here sat Carey.

Beautiful Carey.

~

At the foot of featureless mountains – shapeless, colourless, fused at the hip, mute with pain and hunched in conspiracy – a girdle of shingle cradled the sea. The water the colour of pitch, swum in the blinded agony of fierce reflected rock, rolling harsh breakers which spat at the land – spiteful, tormented, possessed.

Beyond the cruel bay, a steel grey sea, stroking a restless, angry dance to a mirror of homage, a rhythmical roll, the further it filtered from sight. There specks of seagulls swooped and fed, screaming at a fishing smack burdened with its catch.

Wading out across the stones, with trousers rolled up to the knee, in the sheer and empty sea, you could thrust your hands through its liquid skin and drive them up through the spume-soaked air till the lifeless water was cupped between your half-numb fingers and thumbs.

There, captured, it was clear and cool. You could throw it upwards at the skies, and see – for an instant, a fraction of time – its crystal fracturing, firing with life, then falling, spent like a weary firework, back to the indistinguishable grey.

Cup after cup of freezing water forced towards the fathomless skies, charged with the strength of life, of light, cascading into effervescence, melting, exhausted, into the sea.

And here, framed in its liquid rainbow, buoyed by the murmuring, pregnant waves, stretched on her back and looking skywards, floating far on the sun-void seas, couched in its cradle, here lay Carey.

Beautiful Carey.

~

A sheep field stretched behind the house, beyond the rusting tin-roofed barns engulfed in nettles and weed. Past dry stone walls and a wooden pen, wind-bruised and broken down. An encroaching copse; a cluster of bracken; a tumbled circle of stones.

A still summer evening. And at dusk you could mount the gentle slope, the roll of the field, till you came to a single oak. Sheep scattered as you sought dead boughs, and took a spade to the turf.

As darkness settled and shrouded you, sealing you tight in its feather-light grasp, smudging out identity, you could lay a fire and kindle flame to stir the night's tranquility. Faces flushed, intrigued by the blaze, mindless of the blanket of blackness hung around us in folds.

After the early explosion of light the flames died down, and in their wake enthralling embers glowed. Quiet, relentless energy, creating a catastrophe of death and life to dream upon.

Shapes and fables rose incensed amongst the shattered brands. The hero slain; the life regained; the fool who died of the cold, cold heart he could not come to own – not even there, in the very core, where passions are wrought and brought low. The infernal caverns of molten hell; the well where a beautiful maiden sleeps beside her pot of gold. The endless falling through tiers of being; and he who would fly and touch the sun.

And here, deep in the heart of the fire – beyond the ashes and the crumbling cinder – those eyes, those fixed eyes kindling heat, stoking the flame, bright with desire, burning with being, those furnace eyes of Carey.

Beautiful Carey.

~

The room soundless. Walking as if on dust to the bed. Mute. A splinter of sharp, ugly light which slices into the silent room through a gap between curtain and wall. The windows closed, and the air all spent. Dull and warm, this grey, grey room. Colourless, noiseless, trapped in time. Resistant to the force of life. Resistant.

The beat of the blood which pulses through me throbs like a drum in my ears. Here, now, the brilliant day has melted in eternal grey. Here, now, the whispering world has cut out its tongue. It is dumb.

Here. Now.

Even now, I cannot comprehend your strength; the strength of your being, of all you are. Not even here in the dull, grey room: shadowed, eclipsed, and void of life.

Even now, when caught in this moment, when seeing you here; knowing what you have become.

Your nothingness is so much more than all and everything of me. Your lifelessness is charged with self. You are, as I can never be.

These are my words, my thoughts. They are all that I own, yet they fall so short of meaning. Is there no other being? Is there life without life? You, who were all life. All that remains.

Beautiful Carey.

.

The Price of Life

Tears welled in his eyes. He sat back in his chair, scarcely daring to glance again at the page.

The novel was spread out on the desk before him in manuscript form. He had been reading it before the rest of the world had come to know of its existence, and it gave him a subtle but exquisite pleasure in knowing he was savouring its treasures before other eyes had seen it. For now, he had the privilege of marvelling over the sentences in their crude and embryonic state – these thin sheets of paper, smudged with the stain of ink from a typewriter – and of appreciating its beauty before it was tainted by the grasping hands of the reading masses, and the gloss of fawning literary critics who were sure to proclaim it a masterpiece.

For a masterpiece it was. The novel had everything. Even now, typed without precision on a machine which seemed sadly in want of new ribbon, it had that undeniable aura of greatness about it. It was all there – the characterisation of Tolstoy, the wit of Fielding, the humanity of Lawrence, the syntax of Joyce, the intrigue of Agatha Christie. Should someone have been in the room whilst he had been reading aloud, they would have witnessed the excited gasps, the suppressed groans, the fits of laughter which had been forced from his lips in acknowledgement of its superlative narrative and plot. Should someone have been standing close to his shoulder, they would have seen the tearstains on the deformed print, and the quiver of the paper in his tremulous hands as he turned each page with trepidation.

The sheer emotional carnage it had caused had forced him to break off, to shield his eyes, to clap his hand to his chest and take conscious breaths for fear that else he would faint.

He glanced about the room around him. It, too, was full of books. Hundreds of them lining its sombre walls, the random rainbow of their spines the only hint of any colour, the only objects present. It was an honour for him to be here, alone, in this veritable shrine of artistic attainment, surrounded by the acknowledged greats, by the cumulative weight of their literary genius. Here were first editions and rare signed copies; here were books with pages yet to be cut; here were Homer and Borges in their native tongues. And all of it – every volume, every leaf, each printed letter – was gazing admiringly on the manuscript before him, eager and expectant for its pages to join them, to become the latest eminent addition to their august and exalted ranks.

He asserted his focus once more on the text, tracing the compelling path of the narrative that had enthralled and vanquished his mind. The piteous dilemma of the beautiful young mother, struggling with the choice of suffocating her baby or surrendering it to the cannibals; the honourable but harrowing last speech of her husband, as he knelt, clamped in irons and wrongly condemned, at the executioner's block; the heroism of the Colonel, as he charged, single-handedly, to engage a vastly superior foe. The structure was exceptional, the plot distinguished, the style superb, the grammar impeccable, and the novel his.

Yes, it was his. His greatest creation. His magnum opus. The apotheosis of his literary career. Agents would pit themselves with each other for the right to represent him; publishers would vie for the right to add his name to their stable. All of them would see its merit; all would retract the scornful slights they had issued him in the past. Those piles of rejection letters behind him – dripping with hollow encouragement, with belittling dismissiveness – were things of a darker, distant past, and would prove ill-judged in the future. For even those novels he had previously written would yet show themselves to be great. They were just too avant-garde for their time – too original and innovative to be appreciated, too ingenious to be acknowledged. But flown on the wings of this masterpiece, all twelve of those manuscripts that had once been spurned would be borne triumphantly in its wake. Thanks to these sheets laid out on his desk, his lifework would breathe for posterity, arousing public acclamation, emblazoning his name in the immortal annuls of literary history, and fulfilling his lifetime's desire.

He had craved recognition so profoundly for so long, and now this novel would secure it. He had been destined to be an author. An unassuageable urge in his innermost being had demanded he put pen to paper. Almost before he could read. It had tortured him; it had tantalized him. It had forced him out of his job. It had estranged him from his family. It had commanded him to sell up and move on, so for fifteen years he had lived on nothing, he had lived in this cottage – his creative castle – preparing himself, tormenting himself, inflicted by the pain of the punishing words which spun from his mind and onto the page, in the unerring belief that he would succeed.

He stared at the twelve hand-bound volumes on the desk that formed his legacy. For those he had sold his soul, he had spent his inheritance. Every last penny of it. For those, he had abandoned the world, he had locked himself in enforced isolation, fuelled by conviction that at some point his talent would finally be recognised, enabling him to enchant his readers with the elegance which emanated from his pen, and which would alter the trajectory of literary endeavour for generations to come.

He switched his gaze to a newspaper-cutting lovingly framed on the wall. That was the extent of his recognition. His sublime *Egyptian Lament*, published five years previously in the *Evening Post*. And even though the heathens had cut it, and some oaf had dared to rewrite the last stanza, that was the proof he had talent. That was his inspiration, his incentive; his personal affirmation to self that if he persisted then he would succeed.

Not that he hankered for fame in itself; not that he craved adulation or wealth. He was content, in these years of his prime, to focus solely on the act of creation, unbothered by public acclaim. To hide his treasures in this secret temple, nurturing and preparing them for release. But he needed to know, to assure himself, that at some point in the measurable future, the time would come when his works were revealed, when they were respected, admired. These books were his life. They were who he was. The essence of everything that he was. They constituted his very fabric, the being and breath and all that was bound in the body of Reginald Harrison.

Without them, he would cease to be. If they died, then indubitably so would he. He was not a vain nor arrogant man, but he knew in his heart what he wrote was worthy. He just needed to know that others knew it, so his life was more than inconspicuous agony, it amounted to more than obscurity and anguish. And for him, that meant being published. If not now, then sometime in the future. He would stop at nothing to see himself published. If only for the sake of his sanity, to prove himself to himself. He was so committed to believing his worth; he knew it, and he would die to prove it. Though he knew that the ultimate measure of worth lay not with him but with others. And it was that single undeniable fact that taunted him mercilessly.

A shock of lightning spat through the air, followed by the wrath of thunder, lumbering from the troubled skies before sinking, deadened, absorbed in the close, concrete cloud.

He looked up from his desk, towards the window. As he did so, he heard the doorbell sound. Reluctantly, he got to his feet. He shuffled towards the front door.

A woman was standing in the porch, wearing a low-cut sequin gown. She seemed to be somewhat overdressed, given the venue and time of day. He presumed she was lost, though how she had found him seemed equally bizarre.

'Mr Harrison?' the matron started confidently and briskly.
'Yes?'
'Reginald Harrison of Moonbeam Cottage?'
'That's right.'
'Thank God! At last!' she sighed.

164

'Who are you? Are you lost? Can I give you directions to Stranglewell?' he volunteered.

'No. No. Can I come in?'

'You haven't told me who you are.'

'I've got some good news for you. If you let me in, I'll tell you' she said, somewhat impatiently.

'Are you from the lottery?'

'No. Let me in, and I'll give you a surprise.'

He looked her briefly up and down. Perhaps this was someone who had heard of his novels. Perhaps this was someone who had read his Lament. She didn't look like a literary agent, but she might be. She might have come to seek him out.

'Well, I suppose you'd better come in before it rains' he said.

'It's not going to rain.'

'I think it will. Didn't you hear that thunder?'

'That wasn't thunder. That was me.'

'What?!' he spluttered incredulously.

'I used to just appear in people's rooms and give them a private audience, but then I found I was often intruding – sometimes interrupting something quite personal – so I tend to give a warning first. I use the doorbell whenever I can. The thunder has to stay, though. It's part of the contract.'

'What on earth are you talking about?' he said, moving aside to let her in and closing the door behind her.

'I won't mess about. I'm in a hurry. I've come to grant you a wish.'

'A wish?'

'Yes, a wish. It used to be three, but over the years it's been whittled it down to one. It's the inevitable consequence of productivity targets which are aimed at reducing waiting times. Plus planned redundancies, of course. Honestly, I've been campaigning to unionise for years, but I can't get any traction on the issue of collective bargaining.'

'Where are you from again?' he asked uncertainly.

'It doesn't matter. Just state your wish, and please do hurry.'

'I'm not sure what you're asking me.'

'Come on, Reggie! Surely you know what a wish is. Something you want, or want to happen. Something you can't do on your own. Just say the words and I'll give it to you. Anything that you want.'

'Anything?! Are you crazy?'

'Of course not', she replied irritably. 'Everyone always asks me that, and from my perspective it's a pretty dumb question. I'm tired of spelling it out every time. Look, let's keep things simple. Remember Aladdin's lamp and the genie? Well, I'm a sort of updated version. In a manner of speaking, that is. Anyway, who I am isn't important. Just take the sodding wish.'

'Is this some sort of a trick?'

'Certainly not!' she cried, sounding offended. 'This is straight down the line. What do you want, and I'll give it to you.'

'Anything?'

'Anything. Fire away.'

'You're having me on.'

'Try me' she said bullishly.

'OK. I want you to make me the most famous author since… Well, the most famous author this century.'

'I can make you as many books as you want' she declared triumphantly.

'No, that's not what I mean. I only want the inspiration and the devoted readership. I want to write the books myself.'

'Sorry, Reggie. That's not possible.'

'You said I could ask for anything. But you obviously can't do everything. It's a con' he complained.

'No, it's not. It's semantics. I can give you anything tangible. Books fall into that category. Inspiration doesn't. Are you sure you don't just want money?'

'No.'

'Pity. Everyone wants money nowadays. Still, the pen is mightier than the piggy bank, for some.'

'I want to be recognised as an author, that's all. Surely, it's not that difficult.'

'To be seen as a man of learning, eh? Fancy!'

'I thought you were here to grant me a wish, not to judge me' he said, aggrieved.

'I'm sorry if I touched a raw nerve, Reggie. I know you've been trying so hard for such a long time. Would you like me to read out the top ten wishes I received this month to give you a bit of inspiration of my own?'

'No. I want to be an author. It's that or nothing' he declared.

'O dear. We can't grant you nothing. That would set an awkward precedent.'

'Then make me a famous writer.'

'You want it that badly?'

'Yes. I have to be an author. That's my whole reason for being. That's why I've been stuck here in the middle of bloody nowhere on my own for so long.'

'There, there, Reggie. Would you do anything to be a writer?'

'Yes, anything.'

'Even if that means slightly bending the rules?'

'Yes.'

'Well then, might I suggest you nip into the future and pop into a library to see if any of your books have been published…'

'But what if they haven't?' he lamented.

'Then you could just nick someone else's book. Filch something famous that hasn't been written yet and call it your own. That way at least you'll make a name for yourself, and then you can publish your own stuff on its merit.'

'That's not a bad idea. But what about the real author?'

'Well, they won't think of writing a book that's already been written. And if they're any good they'll just write something else that gets published instead.'

'OK. Then fine. That's my wish.'

'Are you sure?' she asked, emphasising each word.

'Yes, I'm sure.'

'Right then. Let's proceed to contract' she said, drawing a piece of papyrus out of the bag she was carrying, and writing down his name, date of birth, and other particulars. 'Item. The wish. 'Go into the future'. Will that do?'

'What are you doing now?' he asked, bemusedly.

'It's the contract. We have to make it official. In case there's a grievance.'

'Is that really necessary? How would I even lodge a grievance?'

'I'm not going to tell you, but you might find out and I can't take that chance. Now, I need to refer to the rule book. I don't often get this request' the woman stated officiously, reaching into her bag once more, and taking out a large tome.

'You have a rule book?!'

'Most certainly. I need to check what's allowable. How far into the future do you wish to go?'

'I'm not sure. What would you recommend?'

'A couple of hundred years should do the trick' she suggested.

'That's fine by me' he concurred.

'And how long do you wish to stay?'

'I only want to go to the library…'

'You don't want to look around for a while? Then suit yourself. I'll put you down for three hours.'

'I still don't believe this. It's like making a dentist appointment' he said disparagingly.

'You will, Reggie. You will. Honestly, you're just like all the others. It's so tedious when you're on the receiving end. And where do you want to go?'

'London?'

'London. London. Let's see. Where's London on the map? Yes, London's still there. 'Go to London two hundred years in the future for precisely three hours'. That's your wish!' she said, repeating the words she had written.

'I suppose I ought to thank you.'

'My pleasure. Now I have to tell you that if you try to stay any longer, or go anywhere else, or get arrested, or cause trouble by trying to alter history, I'm afraid I shall have to bring you back prematurely. And there's no second go if you cheat.'

'Aren't I altering history by stealing a book?'

'I think we can overlook that small detail. Who's to know?' she exclaimed dismissively. 'I'm also going to give you some pocket money in case you feel peckish, and I'll kit you out in the latest fashion so you don't look too conspicuous.'

'All right, then. When can I go?'

'Sign here. And here. And here. Let's have a look. That's all in order. Splendid! So, you're on your way! Bye bye!'

~

And here he was – deposited in a patch of long grass in Hyde Park. He stood up cautiously, somewhat disappointed that he had been transported from one time dimension to another with so little fuss, and that the wish had not been accompanied by some sort of fanfare. Indeed, he reflected he had not even asked why the wish had been bestowed on him, nor the reason that he had been chosen. All he knew with certainty, was that the wish itself had been granted. He was here, in a supposedly known and familiar environment, though transposed so far to an unknown future that all around seemed alien.

He glanced at his watch. It was quarter to four. He had until six thirty at least before he needed to worry. That should be plenty of time, he thought. But he needed to focus, to block out distraction.

He turned purposefully towards the north, to where Bayswater Road would ordinarily be, with the intention of heading to Marble Arch. He stepped out of the scrub, brushing rogue blades of grass from his legs and his arms. As he did so, he was conscious of the rubberised suit he was wearing, which appeared to balloon in irregular places and generally imped his ability to walk. Surely this was not standard attire. Concerned he might be revealed and returned before he had time to complete his quest, he ducked down behind a clump of bushes, waiting for someone to pass. Sure enough, several minutes later, a group of Londoners approached. Reassuringly, they seemed to be dressed much as he, though they were skipping not walking as if to accommodate the spongy vagary of their suits.

He stood up once they had passed. Then, mirroring their motion, he bobbed and bounded to what he imagined would once have been Oxford Street. There he approached a passer-by and enquired where the library was. He received directions and followed them precisely, refusing to allow his curious mind to be diverted by what was around him, until he arrived at the building.

Inside, he was met with the familiar gloom and dusky silence of an echoing chamber stacked with books, with shelves that stretched towards the ceiling, reaching several storeys high. He squelched towards the reception desk, conscious that with limited time he was likely to need assistance. Two young girls were stationed there. They looked up and smiled encouragingly.

'Good afternoon. Can you help me? I'm looking for a book; I'm looking for a particular author' he began confidently, determined to chance his luck at having been heard of by one of the girls before he resorted to theft.

'I don't know about that I'm afraid, sir' wobbled the voice of the younger girl, impeded by the excess rubber which quivered around her neck. 'You've seen the size of this place, and the master eye is on the blink at the moment. But if it's someone well-known I should be able to help.'

'Thank you.'

'What is the name of the author, sir?' the rubber enquired bungily.

'It might be a bit obscure...'

'Try me' exclaimed the voice, in a combined challenge of expectancy and elasticity.

'Reginald Harrison' he ventured, feeling, as he said it, the uninspiring nature of the sound, the supreme idiocy of his request. Sensing the absurdity of such a name daring to aspire to literary greatness. Perhaps he had used a pseudonym.

The rubber heaved with the force of an irrepressible chuckle, and continued to vibrate long after the noise behind its spongy camouflage had ceased.

'I'm sorry...?' he began.

'Reginald Harrison...?!' And suddenly, just from her intonation, from the way she pronounced it, his name bore the dignity and familiarity he associated with the greatest of authors that lined the shelves in his study.

'That's right.'

'Reginald Harrison! Have I heard of Reginald Harrison?! Where have you been, sir?! You might as well ask me if I've heard of William Shakespeare, or Charles Dickens, or Rupert Von Tropp.'

'Who?' he enquired innocently.

'O, you're a wag! You're a real wag, sir!', and the protrusions on her rubbery legs greased squeakily together, in unison with her merriment. 'We don't get many like you in here!'

'Do you know where his books are? Can I look at them?'

'Do I know where they are?! Can you look at them?! Yes, I think we can oblige, can't we, Kay?' she giggled, turning to the older girl who have been vibrating similarly, though slightly less ferociously, to her side.

The younger girl rose, allowing her folds to settle, then she skipped down the passageway, leading the way – round corners, up stairs, down unlit lanes – till she came to a halt on a mezzanine floor, allowing her oscillations to wane.

'Where are they?' he queried, unable to suppress his eagerness.

'Here! Everywhere!' she declared with a bobble, proud of her achievement on leading him here.

'What? All of them?! The whole row?! Did I – he – write so many?!'

'You're having me on, sir!' she vacillated uncontrollably. 'This whole aisle is full of Harrisons.'

He turned and inspected the shelves, running his fingers across the dry spines, reading familiar names. Here was *The Day It Rained*, and *The Hamster that Got Away*, and *I Put It In My Pocket and Forgot About It*, and all of the others he had written. All thirteen. But there were many more besides. Perhaps thirty or forty. All with his name imprinted on them. Novels he didn't yet know. Novels he had yet to bring into being. Novels, which once written, would be cherished forever, enduringly captured in print, in thousands of libraries such as this, for the whole world to read and enjoy.

His hand reached out to a modest tome entitled *Got to Go Now, I'm Off*. He wondered when he wrote it, and what had inspired him. He was curious to read the first line. But he resisted the urge. He stepped away. It was enough to know that he had been published, that inspiration would continue to flow, that his works would outlive him and be enshrined in the hallowed halls of the greats. It was enough. It was more than enough. It was everything he had ever dreamed of. It was more than he had ever dared to believe. He turned towards the girl to his side, seeing her gyrations had come to a rest.

'Is he very famous?'

'O, yes!'

'Literary fiction? Serious stuff?'

'Yes, yes!' she palpitated.

'As famous as Dickens, you say.'

'Just as famous' she replied, delighting in his ignorance and her knowledge.

'And people still read him?'

'All the time. Look, I'll show you how famous he is…', and the rubber lurched to the front of the mezzanine, wobbling to a stop by a large glass case. 'Aren't we lucky' she declared, pointing down at a manuscript, 'we have the original of his masterpiece.'

He stared through the glass at the yellowed paper, at the typewritten words on the page. A shaft of sunlight speared from above them, illuminating the ancient contents. Within the gaze of its dusty beam, he discerned the print of familiar symbols, even perhaps the mark of a tearstain, absorbed and preserved in the aging paper, two hundred years to the day. It was the same novel, the same page, as he had been reading that morning.

'How wonderful' he felt himself mutter.

He turned again to the blubbery body, determined to make best use of his time.

'Was he famous in his own lifetime?'

'You mean you don't know anything about him?!'

'No.'

'But you must do! He's just so famous!'

'For his books?'

'Yes, for his books. And for everything else.'

'You mean for his life as well?'

'You must know! Surely you know, sir! I think you're having me on!' she shrieked, rippling so violently she appeared to corkscrew into the wall, rebounding joyfully back to his side. 'I don't know all the details, though. If you really want to know, you should go to the biography section on the eighth floor.'

'I don't have time, I'm afraid. If it's not too much of an imposition, could I ask you to tell me about him.'

'I don't know as much as Kay, the senior librarian.'

'Just tell me as much as you can. Please. For example, was he married?'

'I don't know about that part of his life' she said pronouncedly. 'Just a minute, though. Ka-ay!' she trilled.

'Yes?' came the answering gurgle from the reception floor below.

'Did Harrison marry?'

'Yes. His childhood sweetheart. They had four children, I think.'

'Jenny Hargreaves…' he murmured.

'Yes, that's right' screeched the blob beside him, 'I remember now. You see, you do know something about him.'

'Did he… live for a long time?'

'Till he was about seventy, I think.'

'So his works were published before he died? He was renown as an author in his lifetime?'

'O no! It wasn't like that at all' she joggled.

'Then his works were all published posthumously?'

'Yes. No one had ever heard of him while he was alive. At least, not until the very end' she trembled contentedly, creating a neat curlicue through her folds.

'What happened to him at the end?'

'O, sir! You're having me on! Everyone knows he was only famous when he died. He was only famous because he died.'

'Because he died? What do you mean?'

'Because he didn't die. He was killed. I know all about this bit, and I can't believe that you don't. It's just so juicy…'

'He was killed?! How did it happen?'

'Well, they found something he'd written. You know, after the overthrow of the establishment, during the persecutions. Someone happened to find a piece of his writing. Hang on a minute… Kaigggh! How did they find out about Harrison?' she jiggled merrily to the floor below.

'All his life he only published one thing' came the soulless reply. 'Some sort of lamentable poem. The story goes that they read something unintentional into the final stanza, something suggesting he supported the Restoration, so they went to arrest him. He was tipped off they were coming for him, and he had the chance to destroy all his work, seeing as it hadn't yet been published. He could have burnt it all and got off with a fine. But he didn't. So they found the manuscripts of his novels, and they said that the writing was heresy. They decided to make an example of him by torturing him in public.'

'You see' swished the flapping object beside him, 'he was only famous when he died. For some reason, they kept the books themselves, and after the Restoration they were published. But they were only published because he was tortured. Everyone knew about him by then because he suffered so much' she exclaimed joyfully. 'He was famous for what they did to him long before he was known for his books. Though the reason he was tortured at all was because of the books in the first place. Don't you think that's ironic? Do you really know nothing about his torture?'

He shook his head.

'Kaaaiigggggh!' the girl rippled earnestly, 'tell this man about the torture.'
'O' came the monotonous voice from below, 'he lasted longer than any of the others. They did everything imaginable to him. They even got a bit annoyed with him at the end. They stapled bits of his body round the room where they held him, so they had less and less left they could work on. Eventually they ran out of ideas. They inflicted all the pain that they could, but still what remained of him was alive. They say that the agony drove him insane. I mean, can you remember what he said at the end…?'
'O yes!' interrupted her quivering companion, 'you must know that quotation, sir! It's just so famous! What was it now? 'I'll strangle my fairy godmother'! He must have been out of his mind. But still, it's thanks to his sacrifice, that now we can read all his books.' She paused, allowing her ripples to smooth. 'Is there anything else I can help you with, sir?'

He shook his head once more.

She looked at him earnestly, before saying gently, 'it's been so nice talking to you, sir. I'll lead you back now or you might get lost amongst all these books.' She seesawed ahead while he shuffled behind her, not even bothering to skip. As they walked, the blob in front of him called out to her colleague who sat below, behind the blinded rows of shelves, resuming their conversation.

'I think it was very brave of the man to die for the sake of his art. I would like to have met him, to have known who he was.'

'I don't think it was brave at all. I think it was vain. And foolish. I would have burned the books to avoid being tortured like that.'

'Isn't art worth dying for then?'

'Maybe it's worth dying for, but not being tortured for. The agony would outweigh the glory. Besides, he experienced all the pain and didn't get any of the pleasure. It can't have been worth it, even if, somehow, he knew his abuse he would lead to recognition.'

'It must have been a very difficult decision to make' the rubber in front of him shivered thoughtfully as it spoke.

They came down a final flight of stairs and turned a corner. In front of them, the girl at the reception desk had an illustrated book opened on the counter.

'Come here and see this! I've found the photos they took as they were chopping him up. Here's a good one. I completely forgot about the way that they peeled...'

'O, do let's have a look, Kay!' squealed the younger girl, bouncing up to the desk, her wads of surplus rubber, flowing, swelling, billowing as she skipped. She glanced at the pages briefly, then turned her radiant face to the man. 'Would you like to see these pictures, sir? They're a bit gory, but they do tell the story. They make me think that perhaps art isn't really worth dying for, after all. That's such a sad expression on his face. Who knows what he must have been thinking.'

Something in the photograph caught her attention. She peered shortsightedly at the glossy page. 'Do you know, I think he looks a bit like you. Was Harrison a relation of yours?'

She looked up, but the man had gone. She called out, but he appeared to have vanished.

'He was a bit of an odd ball' blubbled the older girl.
'Yes, he was a strange man, Kay, but I liked him. He looked so happy when he saw all those books, but he obviously didn't know about Harrison's death. And then, when we told him, he just fell silent. He just looked terribly sad. He really did look like Harrison, too, though of course he wasn't as old…'

Space

'How big is big?'

'It depends. You can't really say.'

'Well, when does a thing stop being small and start being big?'

'When it's bigger than average.'

'What's average?'

'Average is in the middle. Not small and not big. Slap bang in between.'

'Like what?'

'Like some of the children in your class are five, and a few of them are seven, but most of them are six. So the average age is probably around that. If you are more than six you are older than average, and if you are less than six you are younger than average. If you're round about six, that's average. It's kind of in the middle.'

'Jack's almost seven and he's much smaller than me.'

'That's because being older isn't the same as being bigger. Whenever we compare like for like, whether big and small, or tall and short, or light and dark, the average is right in the middle.'

'Right in the middle?'

'Yes.'

'Is average good?'

'Well, average is average.'

'Is it good to be average?'

'Sometimes.'

'You're not being very helpful…'

'Well it's hard to say. Being average height is quite useful. You can reach up to things on a shelf, and get through a door without having to bend. I guess if you're average at everything then maybe it gets a bit boring.'

'Am I average, Dad?'

'No, Jessie, you're certainly not.'

'What am I then?'

'You're… you're who you are. Average is just a statement of fact.'

'And anything bigger than average is big?'

'Well, it's bigger than average yes.'

'So it's big?'

'Well, you wouldn't call it small.'

'Then it's big?'

'Relatively, yes.'

'Big?'

'When comparing two things that are otherwise the same.'

'Two things that are the same?'

'Yes.'

'If they're the same then how can you compare them?!'

'You can compare anything. Though it's relative. I mean, a big mountain is a lot bigger than a big banana. But a really big banana is still a lot smaller than a mountain which is smaller than average.'

'O…'

'Which is why I said you can't really say how big big is.'

'What's the biggest thing in the world?'

'Well, the world itself is very big. It's huge. There again, it's very small when compared to something like the sun.'

'Is the sun the biggest thing in the world then?'

'The sun isn't in the world. The sun is a star, and the world is a planet that we call the earth, which goes round and round the sun. The sun is the biggest thing in the solar system. The solar system is the name we give to all the planets that move round the sun.'

'So the sun is the biggest thing there is?'

'Well, in fact the sun is merely one star amongst millions and millions of stars that are all grouped together in something we call our galaxy. And some of the stars in our galaxy are much bigger than the sun. In fact, there are other galaxies that are bigger than our own…'

'So what's the biggest thing?'

'In space?'

'What's space?'

'Space is kind of everything. And it's kind of nothing too.'

'What?'

'I mean, I don't know. No one knows for sure. Space is infinite. That means it goes on and on forever. Which means we can never be certain what the biggest thing is that exists.'

'How can it go on forever?'

'Because nobody's found where it ends. No one can even say for sure that there is an end.'

'Then infinity is the biggest thing that there is!'

'Well, it's difficult to say it's the biggest thing. Infinity is an idea rather than being a thing. You can't see it and you can't measure it.'

'Then how do you know it's there?'

'Because it's a concept.'

'A what?'

'An idea.'

'A very big idea.'

'Yes.'

'The biggest.'

'If you like.'

'The biggest in the whole… in the whole of infinity!'

'Well, yes and no. Because it's also the smallest.'

'The smallest?'

'Yes.'

'What do you mean?'

'Remember our big banana?'

'Yes.'

'What happens if we chop it in half? What have we got?'

'Is this a trick question, Dad?'

'No.'

'We've got half a banana.'

'That's right. Chop the half in half again. Then what have we got?'

'Half a half.'

'A quarter, yes.'

'A quarter?'

'Yes, that's what it's called. So let's keep on chopping one bit of it, and chopping it and chopping it. How long can we keep on chopping it for?'

'Until it disappears?'

'How can it disappear? Things don't just disappear. You're not a magician, are you?'

'I won't be able to see it any more.'

'Ah, that's different from it disappearing. Get a magnifying glass and then you'll see it again.'

'The knife's too big.'

'Get a smaller knife.'

'There isn't a smaller knife!'

'If there was one, you would be able to keep on chopping it, wouldn't you? And when you can't see it under a magnifying glass any more, you can still see it under a microscope, so you can keep on chopping and chopping.

In fact, because things don't disappear, you could keep on chopping it forever. You could chop it for infinity.'

'Who would want to eat it then?'

'What?!'

'Who would want to eat a banana if it got that small?'

'The banana's just an example. Nobody's going to eat it. We could take anything you like. Think of numbers. You can always add one onto a number, and you can always halve a number too. No matter how big that number is. No matter how small. And you can do it again and again and again. Which is why I said infinity could be very big or very small.'

'Ah.'

'At last!'

'_'

'_'

'So… so what's the biggest thing in the world?'

'Mount Everest is the tallest mountain. Asia is the largest continent…'

'Big, Dad. Big! What's the biggest thing?'

'What do you mean by big…?'

Ατελείωτη Ζωή

He flew down to Athens and hired a car, then he set off towards the Peloponnese. He was going in search of his house.

He knew it would be somewhere in the Mani, and he knew he would know when he saw it. For he had a picture of it in his pocket. The picture he chanced upon in a brochure; the picture that urged him to bid for and buy it – to blow the lump sum released from his pension on a house in a street in an unknown village, a thousand miles from his home.

That was the sort of man he was. It didn't bother him. He was always impulsive, spontaneous. He got into scrapes, but he had learnt to survive. He liked doing things without thinking them through. It worked for him, this mantra to life. It kept him alert and engaged. It ensured his existence could never be dull. It brought him reward, it fuelled some regret. But it never changed who he was. And it would not now. He had done what he wanted the whole of his life; he had put his own interests first. And that suited him, whatever the outcome. That was the way he wanted it. That was the person he was.

He drove without pause in a single direction. South.

From Sparta he continued to Githio, and then onwards to Aeropoli. From there he climbed up into the hills, along the remote and twisting roads, until he reached what proved to be little more than a circular one-carriage lane on one of the fingers pointing from Greece.

He knew he was nearing his destination. He could see from his map he was close. On the slopes were occasional scatters of village, lone huts and tall towers constructed of stone. None resembled that house of his own – that house with no name, which peeped from his pocket, which hid in the shadow and cowered from the day. Road signs were few; they were written in Greek. There was only one sign which he saw in his language, welcoming him to 'the entrance to Hades', down a steep winding track by the side of a cliff, where no one could possibly live.

He drove round the whole peninsula. He came to the start of the end of the road, and began on the loop once again. He drove down the now-familiar lane, pausing beside each habitation, checking his picture against what he saw, eager to find his new home.

Just past the sign to the entrance to Hades, he happened to steal a glance in his mirror, and picked out a track which led off to the right – so obscure he had missed it first time.

He turned the car around in a layby, and steered down the heat-spoiled, worn-metalled roadway, weaving through fields of gnarled olive trees, down the side of a hill and the roll of a valley, until the land fell away and flattened. He came to a natural bay.

It was four thirty.

He sensed he had reached his destination. He had come to where he was meant to be, though he came across it by chance.

He got out of the car and removed his dark glasses. He blinked at the furious afternoon sun, reflecting off the slow stretch of sea lying easy and welcome before him. On the closest point a whitewashed village stood silently, waiting for him. A tail of houses mirrored the cove, tracing its contours precisely, with purpose. At the distant end of the sweeping bay, a savage cliff dropped perpendicularly into the idle deep.

Before him, where the road petered out, stood the only building of any stature. It appeared to be a hotel. Tables were laid beneath canopies, set as if waiting for guests to arrive. Chairs were arranged in careful pairs, close to the water's edge. Up shallow stone steps was a shadowed terrace leading through opened doors to its heart. Within, he could see an empty hall, with a wooden bar which ran a straight path along the length of one wall. A stairway, clinging to the stone façade, led upwards to a balcony which lined both flanks of the house. The windows in every room stood open; white curtains blew their blooms in the breeze. From somewhere within was the trespass of music.

He climbed back into his car. He wound down the windows and cradled his head in the crook of the rest of his seat. He closed his eyes. His body relaxed. He gave himself up to sleep.

~

He was woken by the bark of a dog. The sun had sunk behind the cliff, though its rays still burnished the close crouched village, reflecting upon the breeze-bothered waters, setting the shifting sea on fire.

He glanced at his watch. He stared at the dial, he studied its movement, as if he was struggling to comprehend. He saw the second hand's steep ascent as it picked its way towards the hour. And when it got there, it stopped.

He hunched out of his car. For the first time since he had shaken off slumber he turned to face the houses before him. His eyes fixed upon the hotel. Its peeling paintwork was torn like raw skin from the face of its walls, singed in the twilight glow.

From the sound within, from the movement outside – from the light, the weight, and the smell – he sensed the hotel was teeming with life, as if every person who lived in the village had found a reason to be there. He watched the spectres take human form the closer he came to the door. There were pairs of gossiping middle-aged women; there were children holding the hands of old men. For the most part the throng were standing in pairs, or sitting at tables and being served by a host of eager attendants. All those who were gathered seemed close acquaintance; their gestures and posture spoke in a language of fondness and intimacy. The focus of all was on that of the other. From the sound of their words, from the sight of their touch, came the certainty of their love.

He had reached the foot of the flight of stone steps, and made his way up to the hall. Some of those who were nearest to him looked round with welcoming smiles. Though the bar was crowded, the ranks of people fell back and pointed a path to a table which lay waiting for him at the end of the room.

He sat down.

Through the horde he could see a waiter approaching, making directly for him. As though the man had known he would come; as though he were blind to the many others who had come to this bar to be served.

'A beer please'.

The waiter nodded; he cut back through the clutter of people until he was lost from sight. Then, moments later, he reappeared. He carefully poured the beer in a glass. Once finished, he stood to one side. He stood a respectful distance away, but he did not choose to leave.

'Is there anything else you would like?'
'No, I don't think so.'
'Are you all on your own, still?'
'Yes, I've just arrived.'
'_'
'Why did you ask if I'm still on my own?'
'I thought you might have met someone already. Somebody here, in this village.'
'No, I haven't.'
'Not yet.'
'No.'
'You will. You will meet someone soon.'
'I'm sure I will.'
'_'
'_'
'You don't mind me talking, do you?'
'Not at all. Shouldn't you be serving some of these others though? It seems very busy tonight.'
'It is always busy, and it doesn't matter – my colleagues are ready to serve them.'
'You are one of the staff, aren't you?'

'I am your minister, yes.'

'We say waiter in English.'

'Yes. And minister is the word we use here.'

'_'

'_'

'This bar seems very popular. Have these people travelled from far?'

'They did once, but now they are here. All these people have come from the village.'

'Then it must be much bigger than it looks.'

'Yes. There are many people who live in this place. It is just the right size. Especially now you've arrived.'

'That's very kind of you to say so.'

'Not at all. I am stating a fact. It is exactly as it should be – because you have come, you are part of it now.'

'_'

'_'

'How many people work in this bar?'

'In this bar? I haven't counted.'

'Are there that many?'

'There's a minister to every two people. And then there is me. This is my first day of work.'

'No kidding?! Congratulations. So both of us are new.'

'In some ways that's true. My job is to serve you. You are the only one here on his own.'

'You've been assigned just to me?'

'Precisely.'

'Then I'm honoured.'

'Not at all. We knew you were coming. It was important that we were ready for you.'

'You knew I was coming?'

'Yes.'

'_'

He paused. He looked around the bar, uncertain of how to reply. What the man had said was undoubtedly true – each of the couples were being attended by a vigilant waiter, standing discretely a short way off, watching and ready to serve.

He studied the occupants of the room. Old women were chatting to teenage girls; pairs of men and pairs of women were joined in close conversation. A man who could not be shy of a hundred was cradling a child in his arms. Such tenderness, such empathy, etched in the faces of all.

'What do these people do?'

'They live in the village.'

'And how do they make a living? Are they fishermen? Do they work in the fields?'

'Some do. They do what they are able to do.'

'Then some do nothing at all?'

'Many do nothing. At least, not at first.'

'I'm not sure I understand.'

'Doing things can be hard till you learn.'

'That's true of any new job.'

'And true of life too.'

'Then how do they make ends meet – the ones who don't work?'

'The ministers can help them.'

'I don't mean in this hotel. What do they live on if they haven't got jobs?'

'We get them what they want. Whenever they need.'

'You get them what they want – whatever they want?!'

'I can help with anything, yes. For as long as you like. Till you learn to do it yourself. We are here to attend you, to lessen the pain.'

'You are joking.'

'No. I am your minister. My function is to serve.'

'Well then, can you help me to find my house? I've bought a house in a village nearby, but I haven't been able to find it.'

'Yes, I can show you tomorrow.'

'Now you must be joking!'

'I assure you I'm not. Once you've done what you need to do, we can go.'

'How can you possibly know where my house is?'

'Because that is a part of my role.'

'Do you know who I am?'

'Yes, I do.'

'Then tell me.'

'You are Charles Mortimer.'

'_'

'_'

'And who are you? What is this place?'

'It is not for me to explain.'

'Why not?'

'Because it is hard to comprehend.'

'Are you refusing to tell me?'

'It is better it comes from another.'

'Why?'

'There is a man who waits in a large grey house by the sea. He is the one who has been chosen to tell you.'

'The one who has been chosen?'

'Yes. It is best that you visit him soon.'

'Are you telling me what I should do?'

'No. I am wanting to help, however I can.'

'Help who?'

'You, if you want your questions answered.'

'Fine. I will come back tomorrow. I will come back and then you can show me my house.'

'I will be ready to take you. To take you both whenever you like.'

'Who else is coming with me?'

'The one you will meet.'

'Who is that?'

'Go to the man in the house by the sea. He will explain it to you.'

'He is the one who is coming with me?'

'No, you will go on your own.'

'But you said…'

'It is best that you see him soon.'

Charles Mortimer stood. He nodded goodbye to the man to his side, then made his way through the crowd to the door. He descended the shallow stone steps. Led by the light of the husk of the moon he came to the edge of the sea. To his right, along the stretch of the shore, the grey house stood distant and waiting. He would visit the man who was there. Yes, he would visit. Not because the waiter had told him, but because he chose to do so. He was a man who made his own choices. He would do whatever he wanted to do – just as he always had.

A sandy track traced the line of the sea, overlooked by a terrace of white-washed houses reflecting the shivering moon. It was beautiful. He hoped this was where he would find his own house. He could picture himself staying here. It seemed to offer all he desired: a place to do what he liked. Where everyone did whatever they wanted. He could stay for a while; he could lose sense of time. He could be at peace with himself.

Through the evening air a clatter of voices intruded in on his thoughts. A furious quarrel had been ignited somewhere behind the blind walls. He quickened his steps and walked on. The night was alive; it was charged with life. As he walked down the broken spine of the track he heard from behind more faceless walls the meaningless noise of shouted words spat out in hate through the dark.

At the end of the track was the large grey house. It lay silent and still by the murmuring sea. He raised his fist to knock on the door, but found that it yielded to him. He pushed on it with a finger's weight, and it swung to one side without sound. Within he could see an open courtyard, surrounded on every side by a cloister, shielding the night in its shade. He entered, adjusting his eyes to the gloom. There was only one light, and it wasn't the moon. It came from a table which stood to one side, where an old man was sitting and looking at him.

He was drawn towards the person before him. The old man's face, caressed by the flickering glow of the candle, was creased and weathered by time. It was kind. A young child was sitting upon his lap, weaving his fingers within his own. Opposite him, an empty chair was placed in expectation.

'Is this for me?'

The old man smiled by way of reply. He disengaged the child from his knees, and slowly got to his feet. He opened his arms and nodded his head in a courteous bow, while the child stood rigid beside him. Then the two men sat in the empty chairs, and the boy climbed back on the old man's legs.

The candle on the table before them was the single light in the house. The incandescence of its flame lit only their faces and hands. The courtyard beyond was shrouded in gloom. The planted pots were no more than shadows, as were the featureless frames of windows, as were the untrodden arcades. From the furthest corner, through a veil of darkness, a rocking chair creaked its curious motion, shocked by the shape of a man.

It was peaceful here. The sound of discord in the street was drowned by silence, by the wash of the moon which left no stain, by the gentle melt of the sea. He looked across at the man and the child. Unexpectedly, within his mind, a picture was conjured of himself sitting the same on his father's knee. The vision was deliberate; it did not waver; it lingered and he allowed it to stay, soothed by its sudden appearance.

He looked back towards the old man. Both of them had been sitting in silence. Neither had felt the urge to speak. There was no obligation, no need. The old man regarded him knowingly, with an even and confident gaze, as if he knew why the other was here, as if he knew who he was. The child seemed equally unperturbed, though showing no interest in him. He was staring into the heart of the flame, his lips apart in silent wonder, absorbed in the moment and lost in thought.

'My name is Charles Mortimer. I not really sure what I'm doing here. I met a man in the hotel bar – he was one of the waiters – who suggested I came and talked to you. I can't remember why.'

'Yes, I know. We are pleased you have come. Do you like where you have found yourself?'

'Yes, it is beautiful.'

'Yet you heard those people arguing as you came down the track to this house?'

'Yes. They sounded wretched.'

'They are. There are some in this village who are not content, who have yet to find peace with themselves. And there are others who have found that peace, who have found a way to coexist, who have learnt how to live with each other.'

'Yes.'

'There is much that we all seek answers to. Most of all what is closest to us.'

'What is the name of this place?'

'Is that the question you came to ask?'

'I would like to know. There are no street signs. And the waiter was reluctant to say.'

'It is a good question, and one that the ministers dare not answer. I am the one who must tell you. I must tell you much before you leave. And I must introduce you to somebody too.'

'What is this place called?'

'It is called Ατελείωτος.'

'And what does that mean?'

'The word and this place mean eternal.'

'No', said the child sullenly. 'It means incomplete or unfinished.'

'Do not mind the boy. It means both. Eternal sounds better, I think.'

'How can it mean both – the words are so different.'

'Perhaps they should be taken together.'

'It contains both alpha and omega', said the child.

'Yes. It captures within it the beginning of time, and it speaks of the end of all things.'

'It is neither', blurted out the child. 'This is eternity, not perfection.'

'Whatever the name, I would like to explore here.'

'Yes, undoubtedly you will.'

'I've bought a house which is somewhere nearby. It might even be in this village.'

'It is. It lies beneath the cliffs, on the farther side of the bay.'

'How do you know that?! How can you possibly know where it is?'

'Because I do. We all do. Someone will take you there.'

'Yes, the waiter said he would show me tomorrow.'

'You don't need him to take you there now. There is somebody else who can lead you.'

'He will!' interjected the child, pointing at the darkened shape which slouched in the wheezing rocking chair.

'Hush. Not yet.' The old man bent his head to the child, and laid his hand on its arm.

'Is this boy your grandson?'

'No. Not my grandson. Though he is related to me.'

The child laughed abruptly, raucously.

'Was the boy born in this place?'

'In eternity one cannot be born.'

'But eternity is only a name.'

The old man paused before replying. 'Yes, this is where he was born.'

'No, I was not!'

'Weren't you?'

'No. He knows as well as I do', insisted the obstinate child. 'I was born over there, beyond the cliffs. On the other side. Out of sight.'

'Hush', the old man said to the child, in a soothing voice to soften his pain. 'We must be careful what we say. We do not want to offend.'

'You haven't offended me. You have been very kind. I would like to stay for a while.'

'Yes, you will stay; you will stay here forever. Whether you like it or not,' said the boy.

'He's very forthright, this child.'

'Yes, he can still be awkward sometimes. Though the boy is right, in a way.'

'I am not a boy! I was born on the same day as you.'

'He is right in a way, though he puts things bluntly. Time does not matter here. We have learnt to live without it.'

'Why doesn't it matter?'

'Because eternity cannot be counted.'

'I know precisely when I arrived. My watch said four thirty.'

'It may have been four thirty back then, but we no longer bother with time.'

'You can't ignore it entirely. It exists whether you like it or not. If we went to a nearby village and asked…'

'There are no other villages here. There's nothing beyond eternity.'

'That is not true. There is Ατελευτετος', mumbled the boy.

'Quiet. Not yet', said the old man mildly.

'Surely I can get into my car and drive off to another village?'

'Your car will have rusted away by now', jeered the irritable child.

'I don't believe you. That doesn't make sense.'

'Of course it doesn't make sense!' cried the child. 'We live in eternity, but what we live is incomplete.'

'Then I will make it complete. I will find a way. I will do whatever I want to do. I will ask the waiter to hire me a car; he said he would get me whatever I want. Or is that a lie as well?'

'No, that is the truth. Though you cannot leave. Now you are here you can do as you like. Whatever you ask for is yours.'

'If you are foolish enough to take it!'

'Hush.'

'What does the child mean by that?'

'He means you will learn not to do what you want. Not to take the things you desire.'

'Why shouldn't I?'

'You asked me if this child is my grandson. In truth, he is more like a brother to me. In fact he is closer than that. He is everything that I am. And everything I am not. When first I arrived he was like my shadow; and still he follows wherever I go. For that is something we cannot alter, because now the other is here. At first it was hard to do things together. If I wanted to eat, he wasn't hungry; if I wanted company, he refused. We fought to forge a way to exist; it was hard to do more than survive. Though now we have found a pattern for living. I no longer do what I know would displease him, for knowing what anguish such action would cause. If I took what I wanted then he would have nothing; my pleasure would only heighten his pain, and that would be torment to me. So we have learnt to share our existence, to blend the best of our differences, to unite our opposite natures.'

'He means', said the boy 'that by living with me he has learnt to live with himself. I am who he is – his antithesis. We have had to learn harmony.'

'Who forces you to live together?'

'We do. What one denies the other wants. And here there is no escape. Those people you heard on the way to this house are in the process of learning themselves, of finding a model which fits for them both. They will struggle and fight to reconcile; they will never entirely succeed.'

'You must live with each other until you die?'

'No one dies in eternity.'

'There must come a point when you grow so old you don't care, you cannot resist.'

'No, it does not work that way. The child and I are the same. He came into being when I was born, but this is a place where there is no time. Age ebbs and flows as the tide. The older I grow the younger he gets. Soon I will have my one hundredth birthday, and on that day he will be as a baby – like one which has just been born. Then he will grow older and I will grow younger. And so it goes on, with no end. The only time we sense there is time is when our ages reverse.'

'It can't always have been like that.'

'No, it wasn't always this way. We were separate once. There was a time when we lived apart – when one of us occupied your world, and the other was hidden from us. I sense that was ages ago.'

'Which of you was hidden?'

'It was me', said the boy. 'I was over there, behind those cliffs, like I said. There is another village called Ατελευτετος. It means interminable. That is a living hell. For in that place I had no free will. I was subject to his every whim. I had to endure those things he rejected; I was denied those things that he had. He starved me of hope, of pleasure, of peace. He weighted my world with his pain.'

'Didn't you realise the boy was there?'

'No. Or I would have searched for him sooner. I wouldn't have done the things that I did, nor lived my life as it was. Knowing that he was powerless to act, to prevent what I pressed upon him.'

'You gave him all that you didn't want? Without even being aware?'

'Yes. That is the destiny of us all. Of everyone in this place.'

'Why?'

'Why what? Why are we born? Why do we live? Why do we do the things that we do? Why do we laugh? Why do we cry? Why do we age? Why do we die? What question are you asking of me? What makes you think I should know? You have to find those answers yourself. Here, in eternity.'

'_'

'_'

'Is there someone the same for me, too?'

'Of course. You cannot escape it.'

'Then who is he? What is he like?'

'You should know better than all. He is everything you are not. And at the start he will hate you for it, for forcing your choices upon him.'

'Must I live with him?'

'You have no option. For now he has found you he won't let you go. You will be together; forever together. And neither of you can escape. You must learn to live with that person, your shadow. You must learn to live with yourself.'

'That could take years…'

'There are no years in eternity. There is only the moment; the now. That is a blessing, but also a curse. I cannot deny it is loathsome at first. Which is why some choose not to leave their homes. They lock themselves within its walls until at last they find peace. Until they find some form of consent, some way in which they can coexist. I cannot say how long that will be, but I am close to my seventh birthday, and still I have trouble with myself.'

The old man patted the boy on the shoulder. He smiled. Then he stood, and held out his hand to his guest. 'I do not think we will meet for some while. I think it is best we do not. There is no comfort that those like myself can give to others in pain. We should part our ways. We should each go home.'

Beyond the slender pool of light that lit the fragment of their world, the rocking chair creaked with the weight of a man raising himself in the dark.

The old man turned away from his guest; he shuffled purposefully to the door. The cantankerous child followed his steps with luminous eyes alive with the fire that rose from the flickering flame.

At the door the old man stopped and turned, his face an insipid globe as wan and cold as the moon. 'There is a long way ahead; you must be brave. You must believe that at some point you will find a way to reconcile, and then you can both find peace. For when you do, there is comfort in that – in being with one who is so like you. And then I shall see you in company. Come Αυριον, shall we go?'

The child stood up reluctantly, and started towards the old man. As he stepped across the patio, the visitor caught his arm.

'My other is here already, then?'

'We knew you were coming. Last night we looked out and saw a small boat. It was being rowed by a single man, and it came from behind the cliffs. He was coming from Ατελευτετος, where he has been hidden, tormented by you. We were all afraid when we saw him come, when we saw him moor and step from the boat, for we do not like to think of that place – that place where he's lived ever since you were born, where he has been hidden from you. We knew he would come to this house and wait – he would wait in that chair, one final time – knowing he need not hide any more. For now you will both go forth together, and he will show you your home. Allow us to go in front of you first, to tell all the others to stay inside. He will come to you; he is ready for you; he is glad the years of waiting are done. Whatever happens, you have to be brave. Be forgiving, be honest, be true. Now it is time for me to leave. I am coming, Αυριον.'

The young boy ran to the old man's side, and took his hand in his own. The guest watched them both as they stepped outside, as they walked hand in hand down the track by the sea, till they were consumed by the dark. He could hear the village stutter to silence, he could hear the closing of shutters and doors.

The flame from the candle danced and flickered. It captured him in a halo of warmth. It spread its fingers into the darkness, stretching out through the endless dusk, till it cast his shadow in light.

The Calm

Mrs Pengelly stood by the kitchen window.

Through the stale lower panes glazed with grease, stained with the freckles of cindered paper and the husks of tealeaves spat from the pot, the sea strained its skin to the far horizon, blending and losing itself in the sky, in an ocean of motionless blue. Beyond the wall of the unkempt garden the ground fell steeply away, tangled and knotted with thigh-deep grass. More distant still, the pools of green dissolved into a wretched cliff, standing hunched, its visage haggard, clutching the fringe of a cowering bay. Tapered fingers of fallen rock clawed at the sandy stretch of beach, and were devoured by a hungry sea. To their right, a semi-symmetrical harbour, a neat enclosure, a welcome shelter, carved from the cliff in a curious crescent, fused at its tail with a bony breakwater stretching into the waves. Within its walls, a half-dozen vessels huddled together, scraping their keels on the sand. On the quay a clutter of rusting chains, of oil-cans, buoys and lobster pots. Of tenders, oars, and pallets strung in a makeshift raft to fend off storms. Facing them, over the line of a lane, a bright bunched vein of low thatched cottage, mute and white, pressed cheek to cheek, crouched beneath the threatening crags.

Mrs Pengelly sat on a chair by the long kitchen table.

On the sideboard, just beyond her reach, a half-filled bowl of ripened fruit was blemished with the cups of petals fallen from a vase. A fly repeatedly tapped at the window, breaking the beams of the dust-spilt sunlight straining its gaze from the yard. The larder door stood open and waiting. The plastic of an unglazed window tensed in the unfelt breeze. A tarnished teapot cold before her; a half-drained mug of tea. From the cracks which creased the discoloured ceiling, flakes of paint lay trapped in cobwebs, shivering to the spider's touch. On the footstool to her side, an opened book with faded covers, placed face-down, as yet unread. A pile of sealed letters trapped beneath an awkward stack of files. Magazines still in their wrappers. A phone run out of charge. Spoiled photographs with faces fierce with phantom life and laughter, strewn and scattered on the floor, forever smiling up at her.

Mrs Pengelly lay on a clothes-spilt sofa at the darkened end of the living room.

She could hear the plastic larder window sucking at the searching wind; the sound of the tap which dripped out time and spent its tears in the sink. She could trace the random path of the fly, pressing its body against the pane, striving to meet with the day. She could feel the film of the photographs, creased with the curves of frequent touch, bleached in the eye of the sun. She could taste the dust which hung in the air; she could smell the wasted fruit in its bowl – its sweet flesh splayed from its stones. She could sense the close room closing around her, stealing her, sealing her into its walls. And beyond it she could sense the sea, the endless roll of the merciful waves, murmuring longing, mixed with desire. So comforting, so safe, and so sure.

Mrs Pengelly stood in the hall, in the very heart of the house. Oilskins hugged the wall like scarecrows, hanged on pegs, with aching arms.

Mrs Pengelly stood, unthinking.

Mrs Pengelly stood, unknowing.

Mrs Pengelly smiled.

One with God

I have never denied the existence of God. I simply refuse to contemplate the notion of His Being.

For this reason, some time ago in the infinite past, I was most put out to meet the guy. He was sitting on an ancient spire, and I said –

'And who the hell are you?'
'God.'
'You mean God God?!'
'Yup.'
'Christ!'
'Sorry. Can't help you there. He's pushed off again.'
'O. Um… God…'
'Yup.'
'Am I in Heaven?'
'Nope.'
'Damn.'
'You're not that, either.'
'Then where on earth am I?'
'You're not on earth.'
'Couldn't I go back? I liked it there…'
'Out of my hands, I'm afraid.'
'But you're God! You can do anything…'

God seemed a little bashful.

'If I'm not in Heaven and I'm not in Hell, I don't think I'm asking an awful lot to be put back where I came from. Please, God, just one little favour…'

God looked at me askance.

'Go on! I promise to be really good and…'

'O, what the hell! Let's have your name.'

'Sorry?'

'I need your name. For the records.'

'O.'

'That'll do. Your waist size?'

'It's about…'

'And your National Insurance number?'

'Are you taking the piss?'

'Not at all. Blame it on bureaucracy.'

'Are you sure you are God?'

'What sort of question is that?'

'I always thought you were old.'

'Old?! How could I be old?! Now, what's your National Insurance number?'

'I've forgotten. It's on the back on an envelope.'

'Fine. OK, you can go back…'

'Cheers, God! You're a pal.'

'… but it must be as a frog, or something.'

'What?!'

'A chicken?'

'You've got to be kidding! I want to go back as a man.'

'How about as a Neanderthal?'

'Not good enough.'

'No compromise, eh?'

'As a man I could return and spread the Good Word.'

'Put in a good word for me, do you mean?'

'Yes. I'll throw away all worldly possessions, take vows and live in a monastery.'

'There's no point in trying to deceive me.'

'I mean it! I'll do it!'

'Really? I know very well that as soon as you get back you'll elope with Mary Wilkins.'

'No I won't! I… I…'

'God, you're naïve! I'm God. I know everything.'

'Sorry, God. Mary and I have got something going. I really think we have.'

'I know.'

'What?'

'I think you are good for each other. You care for each other. You have fun when you're both together. Remember that time when you…'

'I'd rather not hear this, God. I'm not quite sure what you might have seen.'

'Hee! Hee! Hee!'

'This is my personal life! It's kind of personal. To me. That's what personal means.'

God chuckled, then roared with laughter.

'When they say you see everything I didn't think they meant… well… everything. It's a bit perverse. Is this what you do all day… sit up here for a bit of a giggle?'

'Well, I drop in occasionally, too.'

'That's not on. It's not kosher. I thought God was supposed to be all good…'

'What made you think that?'

'You know, all that stuff in the Bible…'

'You mean the plagues, the famines, the wars…?'

'There's good stuff in it too.'

'O, is there? You like it, do you? The Book? You found it a rip-roaring read?'

'You know what I mean. There's morality in it.'

'Goodness, yes.'

'If I'd known I was about to die I would have swotted up on it first.'

'Who said anything about you being dead?'

'I beg your pardon?'

'I said, what makes you think that you're dead?'

'Well, if I'm not I don't know what I'm doing here. Why am I here, anyway?'

The room in which I stood was immense. I couldn't see the walls or the ceiling. In fact, I couldn't see the floor. Nothing. Only pure bright whiteness.

'God! God! Come back! Why am I here in the first place? Tell me!'

I sat upon a pinhead in a shining universe, counting time on backwards fingers for a slow eternity. A thousand lifetimes came and went, as measured by the sun and moon, the cosmos and the Milky Way, and all that lies beyond. And then a thousand more. Infinity was a single drop within unnumbered oceans of the stars.

Then through the distance, in my ear, I heard the faintest echo of His voice, repeating till it faded from me –

'Hee! Hee! Hee!'

~

Later on, I came across God eating breakfast at the foot of a mountain.

'Hi there!'

'Hi, God. God, can I ask you a question?'

'Fire away!'

'What am I doing here?'

'Beats me. Why don't you run off and play for a while?'

'O, my God!'

'I'm not yours. If anything, you're mine.'

'Please don't lecture me on all that Adam and Eve stuff.'

'Certainly not! I'm a Darwinian.'

'A Darwinian?! How can you be?!'

'Why not? It's a free world. Well, a free whatever.'

'And you created it all?'

God said nothing, but he didn't deny it.

'You know, I don't like it here, God. I don't particularly like you, either, to tell you the truth. Why can't I go back to earth?'

God seemed not to have heard. He was busy dissecting a sausage.

'If this is your idea of a joke, it's in pretty poor taste. I'd like to leave this place right now.'

God skewered a lump of bacon, and dunked it in the egg.

'I'm fed up with being here. And I'm fed up with you! I want to go on living!'

'You're missing what's-her-name, are you?'

'Yes…'

God laid down his knife and fork and stared me in the eyes.

'Bit that isn't the only reason…'

'Isn't it?'

'No, it's not.'

'What else is there?'

'I think I could be of use to you.'

'Could you now?'

'We could help each other out. You scratch my back, and I'll scratch yours. Metaphorically, of course.'

'Of course.'

'Well, what do you think? Do we have a deal?'

'I'm not into doing deals. And I'm not sure you really want to help. You want to go and play with Mary. You want to be her little lamb. That's too bad. I'm not sure you can help me, and you can't help her, either.'

'What do you mean?'

'Her time has come.'

'What?'

'Her time has come. Do you need me to spell it out?'

'You mean she's dead? You killed her?'

'I didn't kill her. That's a horrible accusation.'

'She's dead though?'

'O yes. Yes, she's dead. As a doornail. Terminated. Defunct. Deceased. Fallen off her proverbial perch. Pushing up the daisies. Humans have invented so many phrases to avoid saying things as they are.'

'Why did she have to die?!'

'It must have been her time, I suppose.'

'You could have prevented it.'

'Perhaps. But it is what it is. And in the greater scheme of things does it really make any difference?'

'Of course it does!'

'Then I'm sorry for your loss.'

'Is that it?!'

'I guess so.'

'God, you're a bastard, God!'

'_'

'_'

'_'

'Still, if she's dead and gone to meet her Maker, then she must be around here somewhere.'

'Why?'

'She must be up here as well.'

'Why does it have to be up?'

'Because if she isn't down there she must be up here.'

'Must she? You seem to forget where we are.'

'But where are we?! You still haven't told me! I keep asking and asking, and all you do is laugh at me! I can't take much more of this. I can't!'

'Steady on! No need to get carried away. Cheer up, and I'll tell you the meaning of life.'

'Please, God. Tell me what it all means.'

'It's like this. Very simple, really. I sat up in bed one night and there it was – clear as crystal, right before me. Obvious, of course, if you think about it. The word God spelt backwards is Dog. There we go.'

The sea in which I lay was immense. It stretched beyond sight in every direction. And beneath me too, a fathomless floor. A nothingness, on which I was drifting, caressed by the transparent waves.

'God, you bastard, please come back! That simply wasn't good enough!'

I sat upon a pinhead in a shining universe, counting time on backwards fingers for a slow eternity. A thousand lifetimes came and went, as measured by the sun and moon, the cosmos and the Milky Way, and all that lies beyond. And then a thousand more. Infinity was a single drop within unnumbered oceans of the stars.

Then through the distance, in my ear, I hear the faintest echo of His voice, repeating till it faded from me –

'Woof! Woof!'

~

Much later on, having lived in silence till language and thought had long been abandoned, I eventually caught up with God. He was sitting on a deck chair in the sun.

'Well, well. Look who's arrived! Have a seat.'

I sat.

'This is the life, eh? No worries. Care for a toffee-apple? Or maybe an ice-cream? The usherette should come round shortly with a box of sweeties.'

I sat in silence.

'Get comfortable. Make yourself at home. This is one of my favourite spots. I come here often. I've got some lotion, if you need. The sun can get quite hot.'

I sat in silence and prayed for silence.

'Are you missing not having others around you? Is that what's on your mind? You're all alone, and you don't like it. Well, you'll get used to it, I promise. Be patient. It's only a matter of time.'

'Time! How much time?! When?! I don't know what I'm doing here. I don't know what I'm waiting for. I don't know where I am. Where am I? What am I doing? What am I supposed to be doing? What am I? Tell me, for pity's sake! Tell me what you want of me.'

God waved a hand at the vastness of space as though it would show me all.

'Why am I here? Why do you ridicule me all the time, without telling me what I should do? What are you expecting from me?'

'You really hate me, don't you?'

I turned away.

'I don't suit your image of God.'

I turned away from the light.

'I've got it! You don't think I'm God at all! You don't, and that's the truth.'
'I do.'
'You do what?'
'I accept that you really are God.'
'You accept me? How flattering!'
'Isn't that good enough?'
'Good enough for who?'
'Will you take me into your fold if I say I believe?'
'O, come on! There's no need to be so agricultural.'
'Take me seriously, please! I can't stand hanging around doing nothing. Why don't you ask me to repent? Why don't you cast me off to be damned? Why don't you strike me down? What the hell do you want me to be?!'

God folded his arms and closed his eyes.

'OK, God. I've decided I'll believe in you.'
'That's nice. What do you want me to do about it?'
'Everything! Whatever you usually do. How should I know what you want?'

God seemed to have fallen asleep.

'All I know is that I'll believe in you. I'll believe in you whatever you say and whatever you do. I'll believe in you forever. Even though you're so damned casual; even though you laugh in my face and treat me like a dog. Hey! Are you listening to this? Can you hear what I'm saying? It's the most meaningful thing I've said in my life!'

God grunted, and seemed to twitch in his sleep, as if there was something disturbing his rest.

'You don't believe me. You don't think that I... But I will! I will! Listen to me, God! Believe me! Please believe me! And even if you cannot believe, it doesn't matter. It really doesn't. Because it's in here now. It's inside me. It's all around me; it's who I am. And there's nothing that you can do to stop me.'

God's grunts gave way to a regular snore.

The earth in which I lay was close. It closed around me – my skin and my body – till it and I were fused as one. I felt I could sleep a lifetime of sleep in the comfort of its encircling arms.

'God?' I mouthed through weary lips. 'God...?'

There was no pause nor space for breath before my cell was filled with sound. A music that possessed my soul; that pierced me with its harmony, till I was giddy with the noise.

Then through the distance, in my ear, I heard, at once, His sure, emphatic voice cry –

'Yes!'